STUFF they DON'T teach you at School.

*Don't let anyone look down on you
because you are young,
but set an example for the believers in speech,
in life, in love, in faith and in purity.*

— 1 Timothy 4:12

STUFF they DON'T teach you at School.

Josie Montano

Lothian
BOOKS

Thanks, Carla, Gabby and Kat for your great stuff!

Thomas C. Lothian Pty Ltd
132 Albert Road, South Melbourne, Victoria 3205
www.lothian.com.au

Copyright © Josie Montano 2003
First published 2003
Reprinted 2003

National Library of Australia
Cataloguing-in-Publication data:

Montano, Josie.
Stuff they don't teach you at school.

For young adults.

ISBN 0 7344 04603.

I. Title.

A823.4

Cover design by Michelle Mackintosh
Text design by Paulene Meyer
Printed in Australia by Griffin Press

A

ABUSE = misuse, hurt

Abusive

Behaviour

Upon

Self or

Exploiting others

(When you are treated wrongly or treat yourself wrongly)

To take advantage of someone, and also to force someone into doing things they are not willing to do. It can be physical, verbal or emotional.

Physical: It could be somebody hurting you physically or sexually or you could be abusing your own body with self-mutilation, smoking or taking drugs.

Verbal: It could be somebody attacking you by calling you names or yelling at you all the time.

Emotional: Heard of 'emotional blackmail'? Well,

that's abuse and it can happen when someone is trying to make you feel guilty or even when somebody stops talking to you to try to punish you.

If you think you might be exposed to abuse or abusing yourself but aren't sure, talk to an adult, friend or counsellor. It's not your fault, don't blame yourself. Just stop what's happening, think about where you can get help, make some beneficial choices and move on to a new world without abuse. It's there waiting for you.

ACNE = skin blemishes, pimples, spots

Acne

Craters

Not

Exciting!

(Pimply skin disease … yuck!)

Yep, once again, not chocolate but hormones! If you notice a pattern you will probably see that your face erupts a couple of days before your period is due. Break-outs can also be due to blocked pores. My hormones have sort of stopped their puberty partying but I still get pimples and blemishes and at my age it's 'cause of blocked pores, which means I don't cleanse my skin enough.

Now, To Pick or Not To Pick — that is the question! Sometimes you just have to let it fester and brew until it's ripe! Then give it a good squeeze from the sides — just make sure nobody is standing in front of you or they'll get squirted. Sometimes you just can't let it ripen 'cause you've got places to go, people to see, but if you pick at the wrong time and with the wrong instrument (fingernails, that is!) you'll cause scarring. Oh … it just never ends, girls! And isn't it gross when guys have acne and they pick and pick and pick at them and leave holes in their faces? Too much information! Blech! Seriously, if they're really bad, you can talk to your doctor or a naturopath.

ADOLESCENT = see YOUNG ADULT
   ('cause it sounds better!)

ADVICE = counsel, help, recommendation

   Answers

   Delivered

   Views

   Intelligent

   Comments

   Expressed

   (Sometimes you want it, sometimes you don't!)

Take it or leave it, it's only advice, it doesn't mean you *have* to do it. And it's the same if you give advice — don't get upset if the other person doesn't take it. It's up to them, and it doesn't mean you are not worthy. Giving advice is not about telling your best friend to break up with her boyfriend — that's telling her what to do. Giving advice is talking to her about your view on the relationship she has with her boyfriend and maybe helping her come to her own decision by asking her questions, like 'How do you feel when he does that?' If she says 'bad' then you'll notice that she pauses and nods and is starting to realise that hanging around this idiot is not a good thing, but then two seconds later she'll say, 'but I lo-o-ove him,' and you'll just have to sit there and listen.

AFTER-PARTIES = (AFTER) following, next; (PARTIES) celebrations, social gatherings

Alcohol

Fears

Tears

Ending relationships

Rages

Parents

Angry

Responsible

Teens

Ill-fated?

Ends

Sensibly?

(The best part of the formal)

Before you rush off to the next after-party, make sure you read the topics SEX, ALCOHOL, ALIBI, PREGNANT, CREEP, CONDOM, PARENTS … oh, just read this WHOLE BOOK (and WOGALUCCIS) before you go, OK?

ALCOHOL = spirits, liquor, wine, beer, etc.

Addictive

Liquor

Consumed

Offensive

Hard drinks

Over the

Limit

(Can be an OK thing if you don't go overboard)

Being drunk is not a pretty sight. When next you go to a party have a look at others who choose to get 'pissed' and watch their behaviour. If you have too much alcohol you end up regretting a lot of things you did because you were 'under the influence', meaning you weren't really in control of yourself; you were influenced by alcohol. That's right. That liquid stuff in a can or bottle actually has a life of its own — it gets into your veins and kicks up a storm. It might help you forget all your problems and you might even feel like somebody else for a short time, but once it wears off you are *you* and your stress or problems are still there. If you are addicted to that feeling you get when you are drunk, then you are obviously trying to escape from parts of your life that you are avoiding fixing or changing, or you might have a lot of stress going on. It might be healthier to try to deal with your stress or emotional problems in a less abusive way. (I won't go into the naggy health risks and stuff — you've probably heard it all.) Hey, and the most important thing is to be really careful about who makes your drinks and where you put your drink at a party or club, 'cause there are idiots who spike drinks with drugs. So hold onto your glass!

If you have to put it down to dance or go to the toilet, just get a fresh drink when you get back. One last thing — don't even think about getting into a car with somebody who has been drinking heavily. Get a cab instead or ring your parents (yes, even if you are three hours late home). I can guarantee your parents would prefer to drive six hundred kilometres at 4 a.m. rather than have you getting a lift with a drunk or, worse still, letting you hitchhike!

See HANGOVERS for a juicier, lip-smacking, blech version of what happens after you drink too much ... mmmm ... *not*!

ALIBI = explanation, defence, plea, excuse, reason

Allegedly

Lies

Illusion

Bull *@#%

Ideal

(Plea of being somewhere other than where they think you were)

It's sort of a way to get out of trouble with your parents, especially when you're grounded. An 'alibi' is that lie you told when your parents thought you were sleeping over at your friend's house but you were out on a hot date with a new guy! To complete the 'alibi' you beg your friend to swear that you were at her place in case your parents ring her to check on you. But it's a bit hard to get your friend's mum or dad to lie for you, so just hope that your mum doesn't talk directly with them! Not sure if alibis work. I think you usually end up being found out, just like with lies.

ANGER = wrath, fury, bad temper

Annoying

Nostril-flaring

Grrrrrr

Extreme

Rage

(When you're really mad!)

Can show its ugly face when you find out your boyfriend has cheated on you. Can rear its ugly head when you're under a lot of stress too. I believe that under anger lies fear and depression. That's right — you may be scared. That seems hard to believe because fear and anger are so different. But when you *really* look at why you are angry, it's usually because you don't have control over the situation, which is scary.

Like if one of your parents or teachers says, 'You're lazy,' and then you go off your tree and get angry and lash back at them with, 'No I'm not!', the reason you became so defensive is that underneath you might feel unworthy and afraid that you really are lazy. But you always have to think of the truth. If you know you're not lazy and somebody calls you that, just say to yourself, 'I know the truth,' and don't react.

If you're angry with your boyfriend or teacher, it's a bit unfair to take your anger out on your friends, little brother, the dog or your hairbrush! I see anger as a useless, destructive emotion. Not only do you get upset, but it affects things and people around you. If you change your attitude and learn more about yourself, you will find that you are less likely to be triggered by situations. Anger is ugly! It blames others. Heard the old *'You made me angry!'*? Nah, that's crap — you made you angry. Yep, you scrunched your face up, raised your voice and lost control. You have power over your reactions. The best thing (I can tell you 'cause I do it all the time now) is to think of the truth and how wonderful you are, and not get into whatever it is the other person is doing or saying to activate your anger. I don't mean bottling it up, I mean not being affected. It's the biggest buzz, the biggest trip — try it.

ANGST = see STRESS *(teenagers feel this 24/7)*

ANOREXIA = see EATING DISORDER *(there are a few to read about)*

APOLOGY = confession, regret

Amend

Pardon

Offend

Liable

Own up

Good will

Yes

(Saying sorry)

You won't disintegrate if you apologise, I promise! You can either find it hard to apologise or you can apologise way too much. Now, if I truly know I did or said something that may have hurt somebody or been taken the wrong way, I will apologise, but without beating myself up about it. Wow! Big deal. I made a mistake and apologised for it. If I'm accused of hurting somebody but believe that what I did or said wasn't done to hurt them, I apologise for them being hurt but not for what it was I said or did. Like, 'I'm sorry you feel that way and I'm sorry if what I said hurt your feelings.' Sometimes people just want a bit of sympathy. But never ever apologise for being you!

AUTHOR = writer, composer, creator

Awesome

Unbelievable

Typical

Honey-babe

Often

Raving

(Dat's me!)

Well, what can I say? We're just gorgeous people who love you guys for reading our stuff!

B

BABE = baby, infant

Beautiful

And

Bimbo-ish

Endearment

(Guys call you this sometimes)

Yeah, yeah, it's cute when he's cute; it's not cute when he's not cute! But I always picture guys calling the hot chicks 'babe', or they mutter to each other as 'she' walks past, 'What a babe!' as in, 'She's hot!' I dunno, this one confuses me. Don't you just feel like saying, 'Don't call me baby!'

BABYSITTING = (BABY) child; (SITTING)
resting on buttocks — like sitting on your bum!

Babies

And

Big kids

Yelling

Sitting

In front of

Television

Torture

Infants

Naughty

Grown-up

(Somebody who looks after the kids when their parents are out partying)

You might see babysitting as quick cash, but remember that you are taking care of someone's kid, so don't stuff it up! I know it sounds like fun and you are not only earning money but having time away from your parents, but it's a big responsibility to babysit. It's not really a good time to invite friends over or ring your boyfriend while the kids are screaming in the next room. Babysitting is probably going to be your first job, and it's a chance for you to practise responsibility and show maturity. (Enough already with the heavy lecture, Josie!)

BEACH = seaside, sands

Bodies

Exposed

At

Coast

Hot weather (and guys!)

(That place with surf and sand)

When you think of the beach, do you think of a good bronze tan, cute surfy guys who run in slow motion into the water (so you have more time to perve) and an opportunity to show off your new bikini (with your new body)? Yeah, right! Well I think of sun burn, skin cancer, dorky guys kicking sand into your face as they stomp in slow motion (wish it was so fast you couldn't see them!) into the water, and having to wear your board shorts 'cause you forgot to wax your bikini line!

BEDROOM = (BED) crib; (ROOM) space, live.

Bed
Expanse
Dwell
Room
Organised
Or
Messy

(That place where you not only sleep but also relax)

Your bedroom is your sanctuary. Doesn't it feel great when you walk in and shut the door behind you? It's like shutting the world out, feels like heaven when you throw your shoes off and fall onto your unmade bed. Your bedroom is your practice room for when you move away from home.

BED-WETTING = (BED) crib; (WETTING) putting moisture/liquid onto something

Bladder

Empties

Drenched

Wake up

Enuresis

Toilet

Tonight

Incident

Nocturnal

Gallons

(Urinating while you're asleep, but in your bed not the toilet!)

Yeah, this can still happen to teens. I have a confession … I wet the bed until I was twelve years old. Don't know why, don't know how, just did, then suddenly it stopped. So there were no sleepovers for me. I can remember even dreaming that I got out of bed, walked to the toilet, sat down and … aagggh-hhh, then all of a sudden I'd wake up and realise I hadn't got out of bed, I hadn't walked to the toilet, I hadn't sat down, but I did … AAGGHHHH! Wet the bed! Apparently the medical term is 'nocturnal enuresis' which just means that while you're in your fourth stage of sleep, which is the really deep one, you might not have any muscle control of your bladder, so basically it just lets go. I remember I wasn't allowed to drink at night and I had to make sure I went to the toilet just before I went to bed. Blah! It's a pain, especially when school camp is on, but hey, apparently there's medication that helps that fourth stage of sleep to be more 'active'. Like, 'Hey, you muscles, don't become so relaxed tonight, OK?' Then, just like magic, no waking up in a damp cold bed. (Oh, this subject brought back yucky memories … movin' on now …)

BELIEVE IN YOURSELF = (BELIEVE)

have faith, trust, accept; (YOURSELF) you, oneself

Believe

Every

Layer of yourself

Is

Enviable

Virtuosity that's

Everlasting

Issue free

Nurturing

You

Own

Unalienable

Right to feel

Self

Empowerment that

Lasts

Forever

(Accepting yourself for who you are)

You are perfect just the way you are. If you feel that you need improvement then do it for yourself and not to please others. If you believe in yourself you will be a happy and confident person who doesn't seek other people's approval. If you know that you're a good person it will show in your posture, speech and actions. Isn't this what your mother always tells you!? Never give up on yourself, as hard as it may be sometimes. Always trust yourself. You are unique (you've probably heard this a thousand times), there's nobody else like you. I think it's fantastic that nobody is like me ... (Thank goodness!

Can you imagine if there was? Way too much Josie!)
Believe that you deserve the best and the best will
come to you.

BITCHINESS = viciousness, vindictiveness, meanness

Bad

Ignorant

Trashy

Catty

Hatred

Invade

Nasty

Evil

Snide

Spiteful

(Nasty behaviour)

Hate it! Wish there was no such thing. People gain
power by talking crap about others and the best
thing is to ignore it. Sounds hard but it's the best
way, 'cause then you're not feeding the bitch or the
gossiper, showing them that you don't give a #*(@
and that you don't have time for this rubbish.

BLUES = see DEPRESSION *(don't know why they relate depression with the colour blue)*

BODY SHAPE = (BODY) figure; (SHAPE) contours

Boobs & bum

Outline

Design

Yours

Sculpt

Height

Arms

Profile

Explore

(The whole of your body and the way it's moulded)

I'm told that all teenage girls are unhappy with their body image. Why? I suppose it doesn't help when you pick up a magazine and a blonde babe with big boobs and tiny hips is all over the cover — ugh! It's the old 'accept yourself for who you are' again. If you want to have a certain body shape because you want to be healthier and fitter and well, yeah, want to look great in clothes, that's fine. But if you become obsessed with it and losing weight or exercising takes over your whole way of thinking, then that's when it may be a problem. As a teen your body hasn't stopped growing, so don't stuff up its natural course by going on crash diets and stuff. Be patient.

I was a bit of an ugly duckling in my teen years (and I have the photos to prove it), but when I hit seventeen I suddenly wanted to feel better for me, so I took on a healthier eating plan and started aerobics. Six months later ... Whoa! I was a hottie (cough cough)!

BOOBS = chest, front

Breasts

Outward

Obstacles

Blossoming

Sizes

(Those two body parts that attract a lot of attention, not only from you but also from the opposite sex)

Eloquently labelled 'breasts'. Like bras, these too come in all different shapes and sizes ... Der, that's why bras do! Your boobs don't finish forming until you've finished puberty, so have a bit of patience and just wait … then you can worry! Don't panic if you think your boobs are too small, too big or you're flat-chested. I mean, what are they supposed to be like? Who made the rule that your boobs are supposed to be a particular shape? Apparently your boob size depends a lot on your family, that is your mum, sisters and grandmas, so have a good look. Well, they probably won't appreciate you staring at their boobs, but just check them out. Also it's normal for one to be a bit bigger than the other. When I say that I don't mean like your left one is an orange and your right is a watermelon — if that's the case you may have to see your doctor! But just like our feet can be half a size different from each other, so can our boobs. Same as nipples … different colours, different shapes, blah-dy, blah-dy, blah!

BOYS = young men

Boyish

Opposite to girl

Youth

Schoolboy

(Yep, they like breasts!)

Mmm ... nice (for you — I'm into men now) to have around. They can be a mystery because the male brain is different from the female brain, and we do think differently. They say men are more logical and we are more emotional. And I suppose that's why we attract each other — opposites attract!

BRAG = see SHOW OFF *(they mean the same thing, although bragging is more verbal; showing off can be physical)*

BRAND NAMES = see FASHION *(like what's the diff?)*

BRAS = women's undergarment supporting breasts

Boobs

Raised

And

Supported

(Yeah, those things that hold your boobs up and help make them look sexy too!)

Love 'em! Different colours, materials ... Feels good when you buy a new one. Come in all shapes and sizes, comparing sizes, D cup … ooh! You'll know when you need one and it's fun shopping with your girlfriends or your mum, whoever you feel more comfortable with. Beware of know-it-all bra-fitters, they pull, snag, tug and pinch until they have your boobs moulded perfectly into a bra, but if you can't breathe or you feel like you're going to be the next magician's assistant and be cut in half by the ever-so-tight bra, don't buy it! Bras were made to help support our boobs, so when we run, dance or walk they don't bounce everywhere or render somebody unconscious by hitting them in the head (that's if you have huge ones!). Try to be practical when you're bra shopping. Don't think the fur-and-lace-trimmed one would suit sports day, or your sports bra would look good with your formal wear. You'll need a variety. Padded bras? I'm not personally into them, a bit embarassing if the pad falls out while you're running for the school bus or your boyfriend is having a feel and thinks your boobs are falling apart 'cause he just found a piece of 'squishy boob'.

BREAK-UPS = falling apart

Breaking

Relationships

Ended

Anger

Kiss and make up

Upsetting

Painful

Sux

(When you tell someone that you don't want to be with them any more — you know what I mean)

There's an old song with a famous line, 'Breaking up is hard to do'. Yep, sure is! It's hard for the breaker-upper and the broken-upped. The breaker-upper does all the foot shuffling and sweating and the broken-upped does all the crying and dying. If you are the broken-upped you may be heartbroken and cry for days (especially when you hear a soppy love song on the radio). It's times like these that your friends come in *real* handy. Talk about the break-up, write in your journal and yeah, sure, cry if you have to, cry lots — it has great healing power. Don't beat yourself up, like, 'If I was better looking …' or 'I should've had sex with him …' and negative stuff like that. It's like being trapped in a pipe — you can see the light but you have to squeeze through the pipe and be uncomfortable until you get to the end. You might go through a few stages, like denying that it's over. You know, 'But we're meant for each other' stuff. Then you might have some feelings of depression, like, 'I'm going to die without him! I can't go on …' Then comes the begging — you try anything to get him back. When you realise that's not going to happen you can get really angry too, but don't let your anger turn into revenge, and don't become bitter and twisted, like, 'No worries, I hated you too, and I was just about to break up with you too, but you got in first!'

Speak the truth. Finally, you'll get it that it's over and move on with your life. Can you both be mature enough to try to stay friends, or has it gone way past maturity? Hey, if you are meant to be together, now may not be the right time and you may both have to move on — you just never know what the future will bring. Open your arms and your heart and great things will come to you (was that too soppy?).

It might be a little hard for the next few months, especially if you go to the same school or bump into each other at parties and stuff, but hey, be pleasant and say 'Hi'. Kindness and manners don't stop just because somebody dumped you. On the other hand, if you're the one doing the dumping, be gentle, kind and compassionate, don't be a bitch about it. But be firm, if that's the decision you made then stick with it. Don't go all gooey 'cause he's begging you back and it's flattering. If, in the pit of your stomach, you know you don't want to be with him any more, then don't.

BULIMIA = see EATING DISORDERS *(a type of eating disorder)*

BULLYING = pushing around, domineering

Bulldoze

Upsetting

Loser

Legal — not!

You are

Intimidated

Name-calling

Gang

(A bully is an overbearing person who
tyrannises over the weak and vulnerable)

So that's where the saying, 'pick on your own size'
comes from. It's true, bullies tend to be attracted to
people who are weaker than they are. When I say
'weaker' I don't only mean physically. It's mentally
and emotionally as well. Bullying is mean and insen-
sitive and teasing is part of it. Bullies come in all
shapes and sizes and they hunt you out to feed their
power. There are many types of bullying: bullying at
school, at work, mobile-phone bullying and even
on-line bullying.

I believe that both bully and victim need help.
The bully needs to work out what's behind their
aggression and need for power. The victim needs to
gain self-empowerment, like learning strategies to
deal with bullies and also changing their beliefs
about themselves so that they don't become easy
targets. Where there's a victim, there's always a
bully. Don't be a victim and you won't be bullied,
easy as that! It's like victims wear a scent or perfume
that attracts bullies to them. I suppose it's like wild
animals — they can smell fear, seek it out and attack.

BUM = buttocks, bottom

> **B**ig
>
> **U**gly
>
> **M**amma!

> (That thing that's attached to your body and is between your waist and hips)

No comment! I have an issue with my bum, so too early to talk about it, probably best to wait until WOBBLY BITS, maybe by then I'll be OK!

C

CAREER = profession, work, occupation

Calling in life

Ambition

Review

Employment

Education

Real life

Society

(What you want to do when you grow up)

Are there too many decisions, and you don't know which one is the right one? Well, the right one for your parents may not be the right one for you. Parents mean well but sometimes they put their own wishes for life onto their kids, like they wanted to study and didn't have the chance so they want their kids to do better than they did. I suppose choosing a career may be more exciting if there wasn't as much pressure from your parents. The best thing is to communicate with them, listen to what they have to say and hopefully they'll listen to what you have to say. You may have some problems if they want you to be a lawyer — but you want to be a trapeze artist in a circus. Maybe you can compromise and come up with a winning solution for everyone, something like, 'I'll finish school, I won't drop out early, but I want to try out for the circus. I'll give it six months. If I don't like it, I'll think about further study then,' or something like that. It's hard making a decision and I think sometimes you need to live a little before you *really* know what you want to do. A few lucky people know what they want to be from age eight, but others don't have a clue, and still don't at age thirty. I think the best way to work out what you'd be happy in ('cause remember you need to be happy in your job because you're there for a major time), is to think about what you enjoy doing most. Like, if you really love animals then check out careers where you would be working with them; if you love caring for and nurturing people, look at careers that do that — got the picture?

And hey, just because you've chosen to study law, then get halfway through and realise it's not for you, that doesn't mean you haven't still got choices. You can swap studies or whatever! Never think that you're stuck. Just remember you can do or be any-thing you want to be, just plant the seed.

CARS = vehicles

Colourful

Automobiles

Rides

Sunroof

(People movers)

Without being sexist I suppose cars are mostly a guys' thing, only 'cause they seem to take sooo much interest in the wheels, base, spoilers and get a bit obsessed with cleaning it ... over and over, and polishing it ... over and over. You know, like:

'Hey, you wanna come over?'

'Oh, gotta clean my car first, then take it for a spin.' Whatever!

CAT FIGHT = (CAT) feline animal; (FIGHT) battle, dispute, assault

Conflict

Attack

Two girls

Feud

Immature

Grapple

Hair pulling

Tussle

Spiteful

(A scene where two girls are fighting and guys love to watch)

They can also be called bitch fights, and they suck (see BITCHINESS). The old saying 'it takes two to tango' is really true here, 'cause if somebody wants to fight you, you have a choice. You either agree and join in or you walk away. Now der, I don't need to go on and tell you which choice to make, do I? Or do I? If you're not sure, read BULLYING again.

CHAT SITES = see INTERNET *(you can't chat if you're not logged onto the net)*

CHEAT = deceive, fool

Con

Hoax

Exploit

Abuse

Trick

(When you lie about something)

Cheating comes in various forms. You can cheat on your exams or you can cheat on your boyfriend (be unfaithful). They are all lies, and who are you really lying to? Yourself! That's right, you are deceiving yourself. You may get a rush 'cause you got away with lying or cheating, but if you get into the habit of it, one day your nose will grow and you will be known as Pinocchio's sister, 'Scum-nosio', the famous female liar who can lie not only through her teeth but also through her heart. Seriously! Would I lie?

CHOCOLATE = confectionery

Cacao seeds

Heaven

OK

Chocaholic

Original

Love it

Addiction

Treats

Ecstasy

(Mmmmmmmmm. Yum!)

What more can I say but Swiss chocolate, chocolate biscuits, chocolate-covered peanuts, chocolate bars, chocolate ice-cream ... what was I saying? Oh that's right, we were talking about chocolate ... chocolate topping, fudge, caramel-choc, chocolate sauce, chocolate milkshake ... Help! I'm drowning!

I'm not going to say one negative thing about chocolate 'cause basically I don't want to hear it, and I doubt you do either! Let's move on, girls ...

CLOTHES = attire, garments

Chic

Latest fashions

Other people's clothes

Trends

Hot

Expensive

Sexy

(Material that you wrap your body in for the day)

Love clothes! Can never have enough. You feel better about yourself when wearing your favourite item, a bit like having that teddy bear when you were little. You might like to keep up with fashion but some stuff doesn't appeal to everyone. Everyone has their own style and fashion is always changing. If you like to keep up with the latest fashions or wear expensive logos and brand names, then make sure you have a job to pay for it all! And don't you just love borrowing your friend's stuff too? It's fun and it always looks better on you anyhow (don't tell her that). If you're a whiz with the sewing machine you are even luckier 'cause you can create your own unique stuff.

CLUBBING = going to night clubs

Clubs

Livin' it up!

Underage

Bars

Boys

ID

Noisy

Group

(What you do with your friends on the weekend)

A fun place to 'pick up' or just to dance, drink and meet people. Going to clubs can be fun, intoxicating and even addictive. But be careful with your drinks (see ALCOHOL) and beware of groping guys. If you go out in a group, stick together. Don't let anybody go home alone — you arrived together, you should leave together. It's kind of a silent code of clubbing.

COMMUNICATION = conversation, contact, correspondence

Converse

Oral

Messages

Make known

Utter

News

Information

Convey

Ask

Talk

Intelligence

Outward

Narrate

(Exchanging information)

Communication is not only important in every relationship you have but also in the social world we live in (ooh, that sounded all serious, didn't it!). Anyhow, if we don't express our wants, needs, concerns or fears then how are people to know what we want, need, are concerned for or fearful of?

There are lots of ways to communicate. Vocally — talking, laughing. Physically — touching, smiling, eye contact, shaking hands. Written — letters, emails, cards, notes. So, if you have difficulty communicating one way, you have a few other choices. Human beings are not mind-readers, so if you have something to say, say it. Don't play games like,

> *'He knows what I mean!'*
> *Yeah, but did you tell him?*
> *'No, he should know!'*
> *Yeah right!*

Don't be afraid, what you have to say is important and you have the right to speak up, speak to and speak out.

CONDOM = rubber contraceptive

Con
On
No
Do
On
Men

(A rubber sheath that the guy wears during sex to stop his stuff getting into your stuff!)

Protection first or expect a present in nine months (see PREGNANT) .

Also protects from transmitting diseases, gotta be used for oral stuff too! (Don't make me go into that, please ...)

CONFIDENCE = see SELF-ESTEEM *(because that's what you need to have self-esteem)*

COOLNESS = moderate coldness, lack of warmth or friendliness

Calm

Offhand

Off-putting

Level-headed

Nippy

Eskimo

Supercilious

Self-possessed

(Walking around pretending to be a fridge or freezer)

Cool, calm and collected. Someone who is very popular can master this behaviour. But are they being true to themselves? (I doubt it.) Or are they being what their peers want them to be (more like it)? It's OK to be cool if you are naturally cool, as in calm, and nothing really affects you. Wow, if you're like that, congratulations! But if you're putting on a 'cool' act, then think about chiselling off that frozen ice mask and uncovering your true self.

COUNSELLOR = adviser

Confidential

Ourselves

Urges

Navigates

Suggests

Empathises

Listens

Life coach

Objective

Recommends

(Someone who you can talk to about anything)

Yeah I know, a lot of you are thinking … *No way* am I going to tell a stranger my problems! Tell me then, are you going to tell your parents? I know you can talk to your friends, but sometimes there are some issues or problems that even your friends can't help with. This is where a counsellor comes in. A counsellor isn't going to judge you, so you don't have to feel embarrassed about going to one to talk about a problem. They aren't there to lecture you (that's what parents are for!). A counsellor can help *you* become a stronger person and take responsibility for yourself and what's going on in your life. They don't change you, they just help you to change yourself by giving you some strategies. And the best thing is that it's confidential, which means they don't ring your parents and talk about you, and if your parents ring them, the counsellor won't tell them anything either. It's better that you're talking to someone than nobody at all.

CREEP = disgusting person

Cruel

Repulsive

Extremely

Evil

Person

(Asshole, sleaze, loser, dickhead and jerk)

What more can I say ... these types of guys don't deserve one more word of my time.

CRIME = felony, offence

Corrupt

Remorse

Illegal act

Misdemeanour

Evidence

(Breaking the law)

Common teen crimes are shoplifting, vandalism, graffiti and taking drugs. Yeah, not cool, especially when you're caught, and the thing is everyone gets caught eventually. Don't forget that there are always consequences for negative and wrongful behaviour, so that means punishment. If you have information about somebody you know who has committed a crime, or if a crime has been committed against you, then you have to consider what to do. Talk to an adult about it, preferably a counsellor or police officer, as they can give you advice about what to do.

D

DAD = see FAMILY (because he plays a major part in your life)

DANCING = see CLUBBING and DISCO (they both involve dancing)

DATES = meetings

Disastrous

Appointment

Time

Entertainment

Sex … not!

(I don't mean the 'date' you eat either — actually that didn't come out right … oh you know what I mean!)

Dates can sometimes be a pain if you don't like the guy (then why did you say yes to start with?), but if you do like the guy, then it's all good. Dates can be scary at the beginning, but the only way you are going to get to know the guy is to go on a date and spend time together. You don't have to do anything you don't want to either. There's no law that says you have to kiss or go any further than that (see RAPE). If you don't like the guy, don't commit to any more dates, just sort of tell the truth, 'I enjoyed myself, you're a nice guy but (here comes the big *but*!) I don't think we connected/clicked/have chemistry.' Remember just to be yourself so the guy gets to know *you*, not some person you're pretending to be. And don't forget to have fun and enjoy every moment.

Also there are no rules that say girls can't ask guys out on dates … so if there's a hottie and he's been flirting with you and you've been waiting ages for him to ask you out, you do it! He's probably a bit shy and is busting for you to approach him.

DEB = initiation, introduction

> **D**ancing
>
> **E**ntrance
>
> **B**all
>
> (I mean debutante, as in debuatante ball, also known as a formal, not Deb for Debbie!)

The debutante ball is your first formal social appearance, and can be a major tradition in some schools. But it brings with it stress, stress and more stress! It's like organising a wedding. Looks all picture perfect, but there's the whole, 'Who am I gonna go with?' and 'What dress am I gonna wear?' thing. The dance lessons, flowers, hair, make-up and stuff. The positive is that it's an opportunity to get all dressed up, hang out with different people and feel good about yourself, then there's the … (see AFTER-PARTY)!

DECISIONS = see PROBLEM-SOLVING (both have to have a resolution)

DEPRESSION = despair, gloominess, hopelessness

Decreased

Energy

Physical symptoms

Restlessness

Empty mood

Sad

Sleepy

Irritable

Overwhelmed

Negative thoughts

(Blues)

Don't confuse depression with just having a down day — we all have them. Depression is when you've felt so down for a long time that you don't care about anything any more. It's like your life is dead. So if you have lost your appetite or it's increased severely, can't sleep or the opposite, don't want to get out of bed, are having problems concentrating, don't enjoy the things you love any more, your school grades are going down, and you're crying a lot — then you're probably suffering from depression.

It's not something you'll 'just get over'. You may feel like everything is so hopeless and unlikely to improve that it's better to die, then you become afraid because you're thinking of suicide. That thought happens 'cause it's an answer to dropping everything in life that totally sux. I think that there's a time in everyone's life when they've thought of suicide, but thinking and doing it are two entirely different things. So don't get freaked out just 'cause you thought of it. Actually if you do get freaked out that's a good thing, because it means you don't want to die, so you then have to find ways to get better. Depression is not 'all in the head'; it is an illness and needs to be treated as such. Now would be a good time to speak to your parents, and if they aren't helpful (perhaps because some people don't believe that depression exists), then turn to the school counsellor. There are ways to get help — through medication (for extreme cases), natural therapies or changing your negative thinking to positive thinking on a permanent basis and helping you gain your personal power. Depression can start any time, usually there's a bit of a build up, then something major happens like your boyfriend dumps you and you just can't live without him. Maybe you feel that you've failed? You may feel overwhelmed with life and changes. Read SELF-ESTEEM and just know that you are a very special person, and you are here to contribute to society. If you suspect a friend has depression and is contemplating suicide you must tell someone, doesn't matter if you've been sworn to secrecy, there are just some secrets that can't be kept (see SECRET). If a friend of yours has confided in you and you are the only one supporting them during their depression and it's become a little drain-ing on you, you may have to recommend they get further help, just admit that it's beyond you, it's not letting your friend down, it's actually saving them.

DIARY = journal

Day to day

Internal

Accounts

Recording

Your secrets

(A written form of spilling your guts)

Diaries are great ... but not when someone finds them and has a good read! I kept a diary from age eight through to age eighteen and I still have them, they're really funny to read. When you are little you sort of just write stuff like 'Mum said that tomorrow we are going shopping. It rained today. My cat died yesterday. My tooth fell out last night'. The teen years become a bit juicier, 'Dear diary, I think Robbie is real hot but I got so drunk that Matt and I pashed (you know … like REALLY pashed) at the after-party … And now Robbie won't talk to me … what am I going to doooooooooo?' Yeah, you end up talking to your diary and trusting it like it's a real person, which is cool, 'cause it lets you 'dump' all your stuff into it, and that's healthy. But like I said before, it's not cool when someone finds your diary … and spesh when it's your mum! That's really bad, especially when she finds out what you did with Robbie the night before the after-party (which was more than thinking he was 'hot') and then what you did with Matt at the after-party (which was more than pashing) … and all in great detail! But you know what? If your mum or anybody else is snooping around your room looking for your diary, they deserve to be shocked! But in any case … hide it well!

DICKHEADS = see CREEP and JOCK *(they're all as bad as each other)*

DIETS = EATING DISORDER *(diets can start the ball rolling for eating disorders)*

DISABILITY = special needs

Difference

Individual

Special needs

Aides

Body

Impairment

Label

Immobile

Treatment

Youth

A disability doesn't just mean somebody who is missing a body part or somebody in a wheelchair. Disabilities cover from asthma, mental illnesses, visual impairment (yes that's me with glasses!) to the physically disabled. People with disabilities are able and entitled to have as full a life as they desire. Just because somebody appears or acts different doesn't give others the right to exclude them. I know it might not seem 'cool' to hang out with the different kid, but hey, I think it's totally COOL if you do because you are accepting people for who they are. Like it's no big deal. People with disabilities don't want to be treated differently, they just want to hang out like everyone else does as best they can.

DISAGREEMENT = argument, dispute

Difference

Incompatible

Squabble

Altercation

Gripe

Row

Expostulate

Episode

Maintain

Explode

Nasty

Tantrum

(Having a spat)

You are all different, so obviously you all have different beliefs and opinions, so it's inevitable that you will discover others' beliefs and opinions are not to your liking or vice versa. That's OK! You can't control what other people think, say, feel or believe. So don't try to force your opinion on each other, 'cause that's what leads to an argument. Just AGREE to DISAGREE, learn something about each other, compromise, communicate and MOVE ON!

If it's impossible to do this then you may need a mediator — somebody neutral who acts like a judge — so it's like having a mini court-case.

DISCO = club

Dancing

Indoors

Socialising

Crowded

Often

(That weekly/monthly event you hang out for)

Cool music, a chance to practise your dance moves, wear your new clothes, and meet cute guys. The school discos are pretty mild and safe and are there for you to basically get together, socialise and have a good time. If you are heading out to adult discos, see CLUBBING.

DIVORCE = split up, separate.

Divide

Intense

Vicious

Overwhelmed

Rupture

Counsellor

Emotions

(When your mum and dad split up)

This can be a really painful experience, but just like BREAKING UP, you will survive and grow and live through it all. In the beginning you will be sad and confused. Either you will be moving out or one of your parents will be moving out, either way there will be lots of changes. It would be a good idea to let your teachers and friends know what's happening, so they can understand your seesaw emotions and support you through it all. Don't blame your mum and dad, they have obviously come to a point in their lives where they realised that their marriage isn't working. It's better for them to be separate and happy than to stay together and be unhappy. Divorce is common now as people have discovered they have choices. What isn't fair is when parents are angry with each other and start using their kids as pawns. Don't get into it, and ask them to leave you out of it. Just pray that your parents remain good friends, because it'll make it easier on everybody. Try not to be match-maker and play games to get them back together; they are adults and they can sort it out for themselves. Just look after yourself and your needs first, then you will be better able to support your parents through it.

DROOL = slaver

Dribble

Rolling

Over

Onto

Lips

(Saliva that dribbles down from your mouth onto your chin then drips onto the ground)

No ... I'm not talking about basketball dribbling either, I'm talking about the kind of drool that happens when you see a hottie — you know, when you also have your tongue hanging out and make that gurgling sound. Guys do it more than girls, and they usually do it in gangs and add yelling out or whistling. So immature!

DRUGS = narcotic, medical substance

Dope

Restless

Uppers

Grass

Speed

(And I'm not talking about the pain reliever your mum gives you when you've got a headache)

Don't try drugs if they don't appeal to you. Put simply, drugs are bad for you. Mixing drugs with alcohol can actually kill you. Sometimes even taking a one-off drug, like an ecstasy tablet, can actually kill you, because you could have an allergic reaction to it. If you're at a party and a friend of yours has an abnormal reaction to something they just took, get medical help straight away, and you could be saving their life. You can always tell if one of your friends is taking drugs because of their mood swings, need for money, restlessness, and a change of friends. Drugs (just like alcohol) can make you feel great for a short time, but the high doesn't last, you come crashing down and will probably want more to climb up again — that's when your addiction cycle starts.

Drugs aren't free either, yeah, OK, the experimenting with them in the beginning may be, just sponging from your friends, but then if you start to become addicted, you're going to have to buy it yourself, this is getting serious now, 'cause you either have to get a job or you start stealing ... not good. If you or a friend need help, you can speak to the school counsellor, an adult or there are help lines you can call.

Are you giving your personal power away to drugs and alcohol? They are only substances and can't satisfy you 24/7. You have the power to provide a natural high for yourself 24/7, because you are substantial!

E

EATING DISORDER = (EATING) chewing
and swallowing food, devouring;
(DISORDER) ailment

Excessive exercise

Anorexia

Tired

Induced vomiting

Nervosa

Gnawing hunger

Diets

Insomnia

Starvation

Overweight

Rebellious

Debilitating

Esteem problems

Rapid weight loss

(A serious eating disorder can take over your whole life)

A common eating disorder is anorexia nervosa. This is when you're paranoid about being fat, so you hardly eat anything at all so you don't put on weight. If you do eat, you feel really bad about it. You might be really skinny and still look in the mirror and see yourself as fat. You're continually stressed about food and putting on weight. You might force yourself to throw up.

Bulimia is an out-of-control eating disorder where you overeat (binge) heaps at one sitting, then feel so yucky about it you go and throw it all up or use heaps of laxatives.

There are many girls in the world who have an eating disorder and don't even realise it's a disease. Eating disorders are really common in teen girls, and it can start out as innocently as going on a diet, or it can be because of deep emotional stuff. Some girls become so obsessed about not eating that they slowly starve themselves to death. People are normally realistic about whether they are fat or thin — you know, it's pretty black and white, but someone who has anorexia nervosa has a distorted view of their own body shape.

I just read a huge list of the gross things that can happen to your body if you have an eating disorder. Things like your teeth can rot and your breath stinks because of the acid coming back into your mouth when you're throwing up all the time, mood swings, your skin breaks out and you can develop depression.

If you think you or a friend are suffering from an eating disorder, get help now. The treatment isn't scary, it's just counselling and re-educating yourself about your body and nutrition. You might think you can stop the cycle on your own, but without the right treatment you might find that you replace one disorder with another. For example, you may have started with anorexia, then you stop that and replace it with bulimia then, just when you think you've got that under control, you become obsessed with exercising, so you over-exercise.

P.S. Masticating means chewing (ha, got ya!)

EMBARRASSED = ill at ease, upset, timid

Emotion

Mortified

Bashful

Ashamed

Ruffled

Really yucky

Awkward

Shy

Self-conscious

Esteem

Discomposed

(Don't you hate having embarrassing moments?)

It always seems to happen when a person who hates you is around, and you just want to crawl into a corner and die. But you needn't feel this way. If you are happy within yourself then embarrassing moments will die, not you. So what if you trip and fall into the arms of the coolest guy in school and everybody in the school witnesses it? What's the worst that can happen if you put your hand up to answer a question and the teacher says that word

'Wrong!'? I know being a teen can attract lots of embarrassing and awkward moments, but if you have a cool attitude about life then these moments (and that's all they are!) won't have any effect on you. You go, girl!

ENEMY = opponent, rival, foe

Evil

Nemesis

Encounter

Menace

Your choice

(Friend or foe?)

Who needs enemies? It's a waste of time playing those games. You have a choice; to have enemies or not to have enemies. Doesn't matter how much somebody might hate you, you have the choice about how you react. If you walk on by and smile, or even just ignore them, then they're not your enemy. They're not your friend either, they're just a harmless person in society. If you react when you see the person by glaring at them or excluding them purposefully, you are choosing to have that person in your life as an enemy.

EXAMS = tests, investigations, questions

Exhausting

Xtreme

And

Major

Stress

(To examine your level of knowledge)

Exam cram. Blah! Just the pits, but it's all a part of school and even uni. Being organised helps. Some hints for when you're actually sitting down for your exams:

★ Answer the questions you know, circle/tick so you know you've done them, then go back to the uncircled/unticked ones once you are confident that you've got the others wrapped up.

★ If you get stuck in a section, leave it, move on, then go back to it. Don't get stuck and waste time panicking because you forgot to study that bit.

★ Clear your mind, like stop thinking about the fact that your three best friends just moved away and your sixtieth boyfriend for the year just dumped you outside the exam room two minutes ago … focus!

Just think, it's now or never, and now is the time to concentrate. Stuff everything and everyone else, do it for *you*!

EXERCISE = see HEALTH *(without exercise you don't have good health)*

EXs = see BREAK-UPS *('cause once you break up, they become an ex!)*

F

FAKE ID = (FAKE) false, fraudulent, pretend;
(ID) = short for IDENTIFICATION =
recognition, naming

False

Age

Knowing not

Eighteen

Imposter

Dodgy

(Pretending to be eighteen years old)

It's pretty hard to pretend to be an eighteen year old when you look twelve! I think this subject fits the seventeen year olds who are busting to turn eighteen so they can get into the clubs, bars and places where you have to be eighteen. It's a little unfair to the people you are fooling with your fake ID, because they can lose their job for serving alcohol to anybody under the age of eighteen. Just enjoy whatever age you are ... there's plenty of time to grow up!

FAMILY = relatives, kin

    Father

    Auntie

    Mum

    Intimate

    Little brother

    Your Grandma

    (Blood is thicker than water ... yeah, yeah)

Do you look forward to Christmas, birthdays and family weddings? Sheesh ... you're such a hero, aren't you? Do you ever think, I don't belong to this family — I must've been adopted! or — Why can't I live with Brendan and his family — they're normal? Don't you wish your family could be like the stereotype happy family that everyone sees on TV? (Hey, what show was that?) That's fiction! Put a group of people in the same house and of course you are going to have lots of chaos and emotion. It's a part of growing up to have different relationships with different people, and that includes your family.

    Instead of reacting to things they say and do just pause, listen and look for a minute. Is it all that bad? Maybe they're overreacting because they're under a lot of stress and they're just going to take it out on you tonight. If you can work out a way to live with them all then that'd be one less thing to worry about, wouldn't it!

FARTING = emitting gas, breaking wind

Foul

Air polluting

Reeking

Totally

Immature

Noisy

Gas

(Air escaping from your anus)

Always embarrassing to girls, always funny to boys! Ugh! But if it happens, it happens. Move on ... literally! Move on and leave the smell behind so nobody thinks it's you! Then it's funny to look back and hear everyone going, 'Pugh, eeewww, what's that smell?' Then they look at each other and start accusing, 'Errrr, you farted!' 'No, I didn't, you did!' Then you'll have to add in, 'Oh guys, like I'm coming over there ... not!' He he ...

FASHION = see CLOTHES *(fashion directs the clothes you wear)*

FEAR = panic, dread

Frightened

Endanger

Afraid

Red alert

(Everyone has fears, whether it's spiders or school)

Fear is an emotion and can be triggered by danger, phobias or the thought of failure or rejection. But that's just what it is: an emotion. You have control over emotion. Don't give fear power over you. Have a good look at what you're fearful of — your dad, exams, a teacher, flying. Write about it in your journal. Write down the worst thing that could happen if your fear was realised. You'll be surprised at how small and insignificant it is once it's written down. Then, if you extend on this and talk about your fears with someone, they become even smaller again. Have a go.

FLAT-CHESTED = see BOOBS *('cause you've still got boobs)*

FLIRT = play, make advances

Flick hair

Lick your lips

Initiate conversation

Rotate hips

Tease

(We all do it)

Flirting can be done in varying degrees. There's the look, wink, cheeky talk or full-on cleavage showing and teasing. Have fun with flirting, but be careful that you don't go overboard and give a guy the wrong idea. Especially if it's a guy that you don't really want to date 'cause then you'll have to deal with the 'let down'. Alcohol can bring out a flirtatious you.

FORGIVE = pardon, clear of blame

Free yourself

Overlook faults

Remit mistakes

Give up the fight

Insight

Vital healing

Exonerate others

(To stop blaming or resenting somebody)

We all know the saying, 'I'll forgive but I won't forget'. Yeah, right! If you keep remembering an unforgivable thing that was done to you then you haven't forgiven, right? An easy way to forgive somebody is to feel sorry for them. Yep, that's right, that evil, twisted person who made your life hell may be a person who is also suffering. Put yourself in their shoes and see how miserable they might be. That might be why they are the way they are. You don't have to be their friend. If you don't like what they do, you don't have to hang out with them, but that doesn't mean you can't forgive them. If you keep going on and on about what was done to you, you become a victim, and you'll keep attracting that unforgivable behaviour in your life. If you can't forgive somebody, have been holding a grudge for a long time and want to take revenge on them, then you are actually giving them power over you. You will always have that 'thing' that they did tied to your ankle like a ball and chain that goes with you everywhere.

But before you let go, sit down and think about what they did, or write about it in your journal — feel the pain, have a cry or whatever, then cut the chain! Let go and move on.

FORMALS = see DEB *(another name for it)*

FRIENDS = buddies, mates, pals, peers

Friends forgive

Rebellious side

Invite you over

Everlasting fun

Never judge you

Don't give up on each other

Say nice (and bad) things to you

(People you feel close to and can be yourself with)

Friends come and go … *seriously*! I used to think that friendships lasted forever, but now I really believe that friends come into your life for a reason, season or a lifetime. I look at my friendship circle and I have close friends who are new in my life and others who have been there since high school. There are friends and there are *friends*. There are the friends who are closer to you than your sister and you confide everything to them and you see them or speak to them nearly every day. Then there are friends who you don't see for ages but when you do you still have a great time 'catching up'. Look after all your friendships, but don't become too dependent on one friend — that's when you can be let down. Enjoy your good times with them, and if something happens in the friendship and it starts to fall apart, you may have to let it go.

A good friend accepts you for who you are, and in turn you should be yourself with your friends, so they can discover your uniqueness. Enough serious stuff! Your friends have to be the most memorable part of being a teen — the fun times, the sad times, and especially when you can be as stupid and silly as you want to be and they still want to hang around with you the next day! That's a good friend!

FRIGID = unfeeling, cold

Forbidding

Rigid

Icy

Glacial

Intense

Distant

(Ice Queen)

Guys normally use this word when girls won't do sexual stuff with them, but don't fall for it — it's because you don't feel comfortable with that person yet.

FUNKY = style

Fresh

Ultra

New

Kool

You

(Like hip, cool, and stuff)

Saying someone is 'funky' is just noticing their style. There's no formula on how to look funky, it just is.

G

GATECRASHER = see PARTIES *(that's where you'll find them)*

GAYS = see HOMOSEXUALS *(another term)*

GIFTS = presents

Gratuity

Indulgence

Flowers

Thoughtful

Sweet!

(Are always nice to receive)

Yeah … don't you get that nice warm feeling in your body when somebody gives you a gift? And especially when it's given by someone 'special', if you know what I mean! Doesn't matter if the gift is something you hate or will never use, it's what's behind the giving that matters. It means you are special to that person. Yes, even your great grandma giving you a set of her silver spoons is a special moment. So don't forget to keep the cycle going. And giving gifts feels as nice as receiving them! I love shopping for gifts. First I think about what the person likes, or what they like but would never treat themselves to, and then I try to find it. Or sometimes you're just window-shopping and you'll come across something that's screaming somebody's name — you just know it's perfect for them. Don't forget to giftwrap the pressie and pretty it up with ribbons and stuff, it's lots of fun!

GIGGLE = snigger, chuckle

> **G**irlfriends
>
> **I**nspiring
>
> **G**iggles
>
> **G**otta
>
> **L**augh
>
> **E**xcited
>
> (When you start you can't stop)

I love getting the giggles. But sometimes they can come at the most inconvenient time, like when the most serious teacher in school is trying to give the class a lesson on sex. You might be sitting there thinking, This is a laugh, but the wrong thing to do is to look around and make eye contact with one of your friends, 'cause then it starts. The teacher doesn't see the funny side of it and kicks you both out of class and then you have after-school detention. If only you didn't look up! 8-)

GOALS = targets, purposes, aims

Glory

Objective

Ambition

Limitless

Score

(Things to look forward to)

Goals are gifts to yourself. There are short-term and long-term goals. You may want to become fitter and healthier, you may want to save up to buy yourself a CD player, travel overseas, go to uni or even change something in your personality that you would like to improve. A great way to keep track of your goal is to write it down. Have a goal book. You can even call it a 'wish list'. Once you've created your special book, write down the goal that you want to achieve. Don't write down what you don't want, write down the positive version. For example, instead of, 'I don't want to be an angry person' write, 'I want to be a patient and tolerant person'. Then write down some of the things you can do to achieve that goal on a daily, weekly and monthly basis. If you want to buy a CD player, for instance, you could write down that you need to earn money, how you are going to earn that money and how much you will put aside each week or whatever. You can even write down the date when you would like to see the goal achieved. Once this is all written down, sit in a quiet place, shut your eyes and visualise achieving the goal. For example, if it's to go to uni, visualise yourself graduating.

If you're ever having down days or think life's just too hard, get out your goal book and see how far you've come in working towards whatever goal you chose for yourself. Dreams can come true, you just have to make them happen.

When I was a kid my dream was to become an author, so I began to write books at age nine and put them in the school library! I figured that if I was an author and I was writing and illustrating books, then they should be in a library for others to read. At age thirteen I sent a manuscript off to Golden Books and received my first rejection letter. How's that for believing in myself? But then for about twenty years I gave up on my goal. I didn't believe it could happen, until one day I began wishing again that I was an author. Then I made it my goal to make it happen, so I went to writing workshops and rubbed shoulders with other authors and annoyed publishers and editors (Hi, Helen!), and I even went to uni to study creative writing. I really, really believed that I was on the road to being published, and I was determined I was going to make it. And here you are reading my book! (Enough about me ...)

GOSSIP = hearsay, scandal, rumour

Gross

Outrageous

Spiteful

Speech

Innocent

People

(Spiteful talk or spreading rumours about other people behind their backs)

OK, 'fess up ... we all do it. But that doesn't make it right. We all fall into the trap of either spreading gossip or listening to it. We know it's wrong, but when your best friend rings you, all excited, and says 'Guess what?' you know it's going to be juicy. Then she adds, 'Promise you won't tell anyone?' So, instead of saying, 'if it's gossip I don't want to hear it,' you say, 'Yeah, I promise. *What* is it?' and jump about like a puppy and think, 'Wow, this is going to be good'. Then you do the 'No! Really?' 'Oh my god!' 'When?' 'How?', add a bit of a laugh and then say, 'Oh, I shouldn't laugh!' Then you hang up and sit there for a minute with the adrenaline running through your body. Your subconscious is saying, 'You said you wouldn't tell anyone,' but your goss-conscious is saying, 'It's too good to keep to yourself'. So you pick up the phone and ring another friend … and so it goes, on and on.

Pathetic, aren't we? So what about the person you're gossiping about? Put yourself in their shoes. Whether it's true or not, it's none of your business. The best way to know whether it's gossip or not is to think, 'Would I say this to her face?' If you wouldn't, then it's gossip; it you would, it's not gossip. So next time somebody comes to you with gossip or a rumour, let it go, don't get caught up in the frenzy or daisy-chain. I can guarantee you'll get such a rush about having self-control and you'll feel really good about yourself.

GRANDMA = see FAMILY *(she's one of the favourites in the family)*

GROPE = see BULLYING or RAPE *(because this is touching you without your permission)*

GRUDGE = see FORGIVE *(if you've got a grudge against somebody you need to forgive them)*

G-STRINGS = *(don't even know why I bothered looking in the dictionary!)*

Garment

Sexy

T shaped

Revealing

Item

Never show

Great

Saucy!

(What's the letter G got to do with a G-string? Why aren't they called T-strings?)

Some girls find them annoying and unattractive, others find them so-o-o funky and cool. It's entirely up to you and your personal taste. They look uncomfy but even I, with my big bum, can get away with wearing one. (Way too much information, Josie!)

Here are some do's and don'ts with wearing G-strings. (The following information is based entirely on observation):

Don't wear hipster jeans with a G-string that's sitting on your waist … gross.

Do wear white G-strings under white pants or skirts … der!

Don't wear G-strings under tight white pants if you have a cellulite bum. Sorry, just not a good look.

Don't wear a G-string if you have a mini on. Think about the fact that when you sit down you don't have any material between your G and whatever you're sitting on — eeeww, like germy.

GUT–FEELING = see TRUST *(that's what you should go by)*

GUYS = see BOYS *(same sex)*

H

HAIR = locks, mane, fur

Head
Ache
If
Ruined

(That stuff that grows out of your head like lawn, and it needs mowing and watering every now and then and is good fun. Can do lotsa things to it and can totally change the way you look)

Oh no-o-o-o, it's the end of the world! You went to the hairdresser yesterday and because she was too busy looking at herself in the mirror, she cut an extra ten inches from the hair that's taken ten years for you to grow! Oh, and what about that colour!? Gross! You look like an all-day-sucker. You even went to the hairdressers with a clipping from *Girlfriend* mag and said, 'That colour!' (And can you throw in 'that body' and 'that guy' hanging off her?) If you're really unhappy with what they did, you've got to speak up or you'll get a sore throat … believe me! Even if you left the hairdresser's with that feeling in your stomach (like your dinner's going to recycle and become a midnight snack) because you're too scared to say anything ('cause then she won't like you any more) — it's OK, you can still go in tomorrow and tell them. Tell them the truth. If the truth is that you *are* unhappy with what they did to your hair, you've got to *tell* them, otherwise they won't know! If you can't do it on your own, ask a friend or an adult to go along with you for support.

Hey, remember who forked over the money? It was you! Der! You paid for something and you didn't get it — so return it. Well, I know you can't return your hair, but they will offer you some alternative that'll make you happy with your boo-ootiful hair.

Oh, and I suppose there's other hair on your body in places where it's not wanted, but we won't go there … it's not my department, it's the HOR-MONES department. You may also want to refer to SHAVING.

HANGOVERS = (HANG) dangle, suspend; (OVER) excess, above

Holding

Abdomen

Nauseating

Gross

Offensive

Vomiting

Everywhere

Really

Sux!

(After-effects of too much drinking)

I reckon the word 'hangover' came from the fact that you chuck up a lot when you are hung over … get it? You 'hang over', as in bent over the loo, throwing up. *Gross!* Yeah, anyway, it's a yucky feeling, but unfortunately some of us don't seem to learn from it! Then there are all the hangover 'remedies' — more alcohol, raw egg, coffee. Yeah, right! They'll just make your body more dehydrated. The best remedy is water, water and more water. What happens is that the excess alcohol poisons your body and the only way to get rid of the hangover is to flush out the toxins, and that's done by drinking water, oh and herbal teas if you can, especially peppermint, 'cause that'll also help with the squirmy stomach. Here's a nice, yummy remedy. The Chinese say to slowly eat a handful of strawberries. Oh yeah, that'd be all right if you could stop throwing up. Can you picture it? I feel sick just thinking about it!

Maybe the best way to avoid a hangover is not to drink too much ... der! Probably the stage where you know you'll be OK is the tipsy stage — stop around then and you'll be alright in the morning. If you continue drinking, you asked for it! And don't you just hate people bragging about how much they drank? 'Maaaaayte, I got so pissed last night I dunno how I got home.' Seriously, that's nothing to be proud of! Losing control of your body and mind is a scary thing. Oh, and the worst thing is throwing up inside your friend's handbag 'cause you got sick in the taxi!

HARRASSMENT = see BULLYING *(pests and tormenters are all under one title)*

HATE = see ENEMY *(they usually hate you)*

HEALTH = fitness, vitality

Heart

Energy

Active

Life

Thrive

Hardy

(Should be a No. 1 priority)

Our bodies were made to move and wobble! It's important that you do some form of exercise at least three times a week, and that doesn't mean standing up to change the TV channel or walking from the bus stop into school. Try to look after your physical, mental and spiritual sides to keep a healthy balance.

Physical: Choose nutritious foods, eliminate snacks. Drink heaps and heaps of water — it flushes everything out! To keep your heart fit, you need to exercise for at least twenty minutes nonstop. So if your friend lives twenty minutes away, start walking!

Mental: Try to keep your stress levels down by being organised. Think positive thoughts and smile!

Spiritual: Spend time with yourself, burn some incense, meditate or pray — whatever helps you unwind and be still.

HEARTBREAK = see BREAK-UPS *(that's what it feels like when you break up 8-( )*

HEIGHT = see BODY SHAPE *(I suppose length is a shape!)*

HICKEY = like it's going to be in the dictionary!

Hidden

Imprint

Cover up

Kissing

Embarrassing

You'll regret it

(Lovebite)

Nearly everyone gets or gives a love bite at some stage in their lives. It can be fun while it's happening, but then the next morning when you look in the mirror and you've got these coin-sized bruises all over your neck and your mum is knocking on the bathroom door 'cause she wants to come in ... aagghhhh! What now? Emergency!

Here are some quick hints:

★ Grab your cover-up stick and go to work.

★ If it's winter you can wear a high-necked jumper or a scarf.

★ If it's summer you can wear a wide choker.

Some people don't care and don't do any of the above, but they become a walking advertisement that they made out or had sex the night before. The choice is yours.

HIPS = flanks, sides

Have

Immense

Pleasure

Swinging!

(Those parts of the body on either side, below the waist, above the thighs — hard to describe!)

Yeah, so, what about them? I suppose you just hate chicks who have no hips? 'Cause they can fit into smaller sizes! But I'm not sure if guys like that or not. I think some guys like girls with a bit of curve. But then who cares if guys like it or not? Why don't they go and look at their own hips!

HOLIDAY = vacation, rest, time-off

Hotels

Overseas

Leave

Itinerary

Depart

Away

Yay!

(Sand, sun and surf)

Agghhhh ... I feel relaxed already. Don't you just love holidays? If you're lucky enough your family goes away every year to somewhere exotic, while we all stay behind and fill out crosswords! Look out for that holiday romance!

HOMEWORK = lessons, studies

Hell

Over

Maths

Endless

Writing

On weekends too!

Ritual

Knowledge

(Schoolwork done at home … sux!)

Work should be for school, and home should be for rest. But hey, that's life. It's something that you *have* to do. The only way I used to get through homework was to do it in front of the TV or get together with a friend on the weekend and have heaps of fun in between maths sums. I think the idea behind it is to get you used to university.

I reckon having homework starts bad habits for your adult years. Imagine bringing work home every night! (Actually, some people do.) You've got to get a life!

HOMOSEXUAL = (HOMO) same; (SEXUAL) intimate

Honesty

Owe

Myself

Opposite

Sex

Expression

Xploring

Understanding

Acceptance

Lesbian/Gay

(Sexually attracted to members of the same sex)

If you're confused about your sexuality, that's OK, don't stress about it. Take the time to think about it and discover who you really are. If you're worried about being homosexual (or even bi-sexual, which is when you are attracted to both males and females) and not being accepted by your peers, friends or family, then you have to make a decision. If you pretend you are somebody you are not now, you'll find that you'll keep pretending for the rest of your life.

Not only will you be deceiving yourself but also the people you have relationships with. Yes, if you 'come out' with your truth you may upset some people and even lose some friends, but hey, if you're happy being who you are, who gives a rat's about the people who don't approve of you? They obviously have hang-ups of their own — and do you really want to hang out with people like that? You'll end up opening doors for new friendships and, you know what? You'll be OK.

HORMONES = chemicals released by glands

Headaches

Overactive

Raging

Mood swings

Oestrogen

Natural

Emotional

Sleeplessness

(These things that have huge parties in our body)

Are just annoying little things that give your body signals to change. I mean, can't we just wake up one morning and poof! There you have it — you're a grown up! Why do we have to go through the acne, puberty, mood swings and stuff? Hormones are not only responsible for your physical changes but also for your emotional state. They can make you do silly things or react differently or have feelings that don't match with the situation, such as crying for no reason. But to explain it logically, hormones are substances that are released via our glands, so they're not imaginary, they actually do play a major part in our lives.

HYGIENE = see ODOUR *(bad hygiene makes stinky smells)*

I

ILLEGAL ACTION = see CRIME
(consequences for both)

IMMATURITY = prematurity, juvenility

Infant

Mature

Mood

Adolescent

Teen

Unripe

Raw

Inexperienced

Transforming

Young

(Childish)

Don't you just hate immature guys? I'm talking about guys your own age and how they act like eight-year-olds sometimes, so not cool. But you have to remember that everyone matures at a different rate, so there's going to be guys of the same age out there, some of whom are mature and others who aren't!

The fact is that girls sort of mature a bit faster than guys in the teen years, so there's a gap that becomes noticeable. Just ride it out — they'll eventually catch up … I think!

INDIVIDUAL = see BELIEVE IN YOURSELF
(believe you're an individual)

INTERNET = worldwide electronic communication source

Interpersonal

Navigate

Terminals

Email

Roam

Net

Emoticons

Tool-bars

(The world at your fingertips)

I can't imagine life without the Internet now. But a warning, there is just as much bad stuff on the Internet as good. Good = Chat sites, research, email and heaps of stuff. Bad = cyber predators (stalkers), pornography, spam, hackers. Don't automatically believe that the guy from another country you are chatting with is 'blond, tall, gorgeous and sixteen'. He could be an overweight fifty year old sitting behind a computer screen having a great time fooling you ... horrible thought! I know you get the gist of it: don't give out personal information, blah, blah, but seriously, *don't give out personal information!* Be broad with the information you give, like when they say, 'Where do you live?', don't say, '591732 Main Rd, Cybertown', just give them the city you live in. Some stalkers are very good at getting information out of you and before you know it they know what school you're at, who your friends are and what lipstick you like to wear!

If you're having a problem with someone annoying you on a chat site, just 'block' them. If it continues there's heaps of help on the net, like the Internet Police and the Net Angels. Anyhow, enough scary lecturing. Chat sites can be fun too.

J

JEALOUSY = resentment

Just

Envy

Anger

Losin' it

Outrage

Upset

Spiteful

You!

(To be green with envy — not a pretty sight, and it doesn't match your hair!)

Jealousy is about *you*, not the other person. If you are really competitive and don't feel worthy, then when somebody else achieves something, even if it's your best friend, you will feel that tinge of jealousy because you wanted to achieve it for yourself.

Basically, if you are an insecure person, you will look for the negative in a situation.

Here's how you can test if you're insecure. Say you see your boyfriend talking to another girl (who just happens to be the new gorgeous girl who does modelling part-time), if your face automatically starts to become a hazy green and you think, What are they doing? and then glare in their direction; or you think, Bitch, she's after him! and walk off in a huff or, even worse, run over, throw her to the ground and pull tufts of her beautiful model's hair out (and she won't be able to model for the next sixteen years, he he), then you are insecure!

If you think, Gotta keep them apart no matter what 'cause he might get to like her, run over to them in slow motion, throw her aside and give him a big pash, then frankly, my dear, you are insecure!

Alternatively, picture the same situation (remember gorgeous modelling girl). If you think, Oh, there's Brad talking to that gorgeous girl. I'll go over and introduce myself and tell her how beautiful she is, then you are not insecure — you are one in a million and I just don't think you exist! Nah, seriously, being insecure just means that you don't think you're worthy or you don't love yourself enough. I know all this sounds a bit corny but it's true. If you feel completely good about yourself then you'll feel OK about your boyfriend talking to other girls. Even if he runs away with one of them, you know that you'll be OK, because you have yourself, you are a beautiful person and somebody better than Brad will come along and sweep you off your feet anyhow! (Hey, did any of that make sense? I'll have to talk to my editor about how I just ramble on and on and on … on … on.)

JERKS = see JOCK or CREEP *(same types)*

JOB = task, work

Junior

Occupation

Boss

(You need one to make money)

The type of job I'm talking about isn't your future career, but a part-time job that is easy to do and pays you regularly. Like working in a fastfood store, clothing shop or supermarket. Some people love going to their job because they get to socialise, dress up and meet people. But hey, you don't have to have a job you know. The timing might not be right, especially if you've got heaps of school work and couldn't cope with the responsibility of a job, a boss and work colleagues. If you *really* need the money, though, to pay for all those extra expenses that your parents won't pay then start looking.

Before you start applying for jobs, make sure you have a resume. A resume is information about you and your experiences which you give to potential employers. You should learn about resumes at school. If you need help writing one, talk to your careers counsellor or your parents.

JOCK = (not in my dictionary)

Jerks

One-sided

Conventional

Ken dolls

(A male wannabe)

Jocks are idiots who dress the same, act like Ken dolls, go to posh private schools, have mountains of pocket money, are intolerant of difference, whose only worry is what colour sports car they'll be buying and who wouldn't know a global news event if it slapped them right in the face.

JUNK FOOD = (JUNK) trash, rubbish; (FOOD) edibles

Just

Useless

Nasty

Kitsch food

Fries

Overdone

Oily

Dodgy

(Evil because it's very fatty, but it tastes so good!)

We all eat it, we all love it and yet we *know* it's not good for us.

I don't need to rave on here. I suppose if you look at the meaning of the two words, JUNK and FOOD, you get 'trash edibles', so basically they're telling us we're eating rubbish and we know it. And keep doing it … sigh!

K

KISSING = embracing, lips touching

Kiss
Intimate
Sloppy
Slobbery
Initiate
Nuzzle
Getting with

(Making out)

Sloppy kisses, *bad!* Gentle kisses, *good!* Kissing is a passionate way of expressing how you feel about someone you like (that's probably why it's also called 'pashing'). The problem with kissing is that girls love it and can do it for hours and be happy with just that, whereas guys love it but after about two minutes they get a message from 'downstairs' saying, 'That's enough kissing, what about me?'

Don't panic too much about kissing if you haven't kissed anybody before. Just plant your lips on his gently, and let it happen naturally. If he's a bit of a slobberer and seems to be cleaning your face like a cat cleans her kittens, just push him away gently and say something like (well, whisper, 'cause it's always more romantic), 'I like it when you kiss me gently … on the lips'. Don't say, 'Oh gross!' yet — give him another chance. Then if he doesn't get the hint and continues to give your face a super-cleanse, *then* you can push him away and say, '*Gross*, I'll have to get my face dry-cleaned now!' and maybe he'll get the hint. Let him go practise on some other bunny, 'cause you'll be all 'washed out'!

L

LONELY = isolated, unhappily alone, single

Loss
Only
Nobody
Exclusive
Longing
Yourself

(When you feel all alone)

It is sometimes nice to be alone and have your own space and quiet time. Actually it's really healthy to do this for yourself, as you are an individual and your individuality needs feeding. But there are times when you crave company. Instead of sitting in your room sulking, get on the phone and ring your friends, organise a spontaneous outing. Or hang out with whoever is in the house — yes, it could be your mum, dad or little brother. Hey, you might have fun with them! Go have coffee with your mum. Watch a video with your dad. Go outside and play with your brother. I know it might not sound cool, but who gives a #*@, just give it a go, you might be surprised.

Sometimes loneliness can be a real problem and a major part of DEPRESSION and people can turn to DRUGS to replace the feelings of fun that company can give. But like I said earlier, if you can feed your loneliness by enjoying your own company then you've got it made, 'cause you are a portable companion who goes everywhere with you!

LOVE = be fond of, be devoted to, adore

Liking

Object

Value

Emotion

(When your heart skips a beat)

What is love? It's a question that has been asked for centuries. Some people think that love doesn't exist, but it does. Love is like a rainbow and the seven colours are the different degrees of the emotion — love for your parents, love for grandma, love for your pet, love for your best friends and love for your boyfriend. I think love is when you care deeply for an individual and respect them highly and, particularly with boyfriends, you may have an unexplained connection. Don't mistake the initial heart palpitations and infatuation of a crush with love. I always like to think if, after about six months, you are still together and things are going well, then you could be on the road to love-dom.

If you are in love with somebody else and they don't reciprocate those feelings, you can't make them love you. Just let it go — see BREAK-UPS. So yeah ... what is love?

LIES = see CHEAT and TRUTH (Pinocchio's way
   of life)

M

MAKE-UP = cosmetics

Mascara

Artist

Kissable lipstick

Eye shadow

Undercover

Powder

(Face painting)

Is great for bringing out the good features of your face or to cover up pimples. Is good if you don't overuse it. Something that a lot of girls and women just can't live without. There are so many hints and tricks with make-up but hey, don't spend half your life in front of that mirror trying to apply it — get out there and have fun! You can practise on each other, learn from magazines or, if you're really serious, you could do a course in the school holidays and learn more about your skin and make-up. I personally prefer the natural look, so I only wear lipstick every day. I save my mascara and a little eye shadow for when I go out. I feel that if I wore make-up every day I would look the same day-in, day-out, unless I was really clever and could paint on five different looks! Now that's creative!

If you do choose to wear make-up a lot you should also be choosing to cleanse your face every day. Makes sense — putting creams and powders on to your skin, skin soaks them up, blocks, pimples, blah! Instead, put creams and powders on to skin, cleanse to remove all make-up, clean skin, no pimples!

Some people use make-up to mask their faces. Hmmmm, you may have to read SELF-ESTEEM. Now, going to a party is different, make-up galore! Glitter not only on your face, but on your body, little stars around the eyes, glitter lip-gloss, yeah … you go, girl!

MAKING OUT = see KISSING *(mmmmm, kissing leads to making out)*

MALE BODY = (MALE) manly, masculine; (BODY) figure, physique

Muscles

Abs

Let's

Enjoy

Butts

Okay

Dynamic &

Yummy!

(Mmmmmmmm! Very nice … Stop it!)

I suppose I can talk about how guys have different bodies (like they know this stuff already, Josie) and that they develop differently to us and they too have major concerns about their bodies … (and your point?) and they've got different parts to females … (groan)! OK, settle down! There's not much to say here — we can all be honest … we like!

MALE MATES = (MALE) masculine, boy, guy; (MATES) companions, friends

Male

Advice

Legitimate

Experts

Movies

Awesome

Talks

Eliminate

Sex

(Friends that are guys!)

Are awesome 'cause you get a guy's point of view on everything, and can be a good mate without any bitchiness. Although sometimes parents overlook the friendship and put the words 'boy' and 'friend' together to make one word and they assume you're an item.

Sometimes it's easier to have a male mate than a female mate. I don't know why, it just is. You may find you have a bond with a guy but it's not a dating bond, if you know what I mean. It can come in real handy having a male mate, especially when you need boyfriend advice. But you have to have an understanding boyfriend (and parents) if you are going to keep your friendship going with your male mate, because a lot of guys (and parents) can't understand how you can have a guy as a best friend. Hey, if you end up falling for your male mate and he falls for you, then that's even better 'cause your relationship will be based on a strong friendship. Go for it!

MARRIAGE = matrimony, wedding

Match

Attach

Rings

Rice throwing

Invitations

Attendants

Guests

Eternal

(Don't even think of it … at your age, anyhow!)

You may think you're ready for marriage, but are you? Are you marrying for the wrong reasons? Because you are pregnant? Because you don't want to lose the guy? Because you want to escape your home life? Because it's a tradition in your family to marry young? I was a teen when I married and I wouldn't recommend it — marrying as a teen that is! I wish that I'd finished developing as a teenager, finished becoming who I really was and set out on heaps of worldly adventures then, when I'd come full circle and it's like, well, what now?, then I may have felt ready to marry and settle down. You will know in your heart when you are truly ready. If you are having doubts, don't do it. Don't be pressured by anybody, do what is right for you.

On a brighter note, weddings can be cool to go to … that's other people's weddings! And it can be even cooler if your mum or dad are getting married again — you get to be a part of the celebrations and planning.

MASTICATING = see EATING DISORDER
(look it up in the dictionary, 'cause it's not what you think!)

MEDIATION = see DISAGREEMENT *(is needed to help patch up a disagreement)*

MIRROR = looking glass, copy, reflect

My
Image
Ricocheted
Reversed
Or
Reflected

(Where that other you lives)

Now we can spend a ridiculous amount of time in front of this piece of glass, turn this way to look at your shoes, turn that way to look at your boobs, turn around to check out your bum — it goes on and on and on. Then come the close-ups — do you really have to bump your nose onto the glass to check out the pimple on your chin? And let's not mention the make-up! Where would you be without a mirror to put on your make-up? Your face would look like your two-year-old sister had done it for you! Don't you just hate the mirrors in shop change rooms? Why do they make us look three sizes bigger? You would think they'd be the opposite so we'd look in the mirror, decide we look great and buy the stuff!

Mirrors are very good for self-esteem exercises (see SELF-ESTEEM) so make sure you have one in your room.

MISTAKES = see APOLOGY *('cause after you make one, you have to make the other)*

MOBILE PHONE = (MOBILE) moveable, travelling; (PHONE) communication device

Movable

Obsessed

Bills!

Incoming call

Line

Entertaining

Portable

Hi!

Outgoing call

Nuisance

Emoticons

(Communication things that we can't live without!)

It's cool to have one and all, but being on it 24/7 and *at school* makes you look like a complete wannabe. It's fun with the cute covers, and SMSing. But who pays the bills? See JOB!

MONEY = banknotes, cash

More

Of

Never

Enough

You need it

(Money makes the world go around)

You can get anything with it — well that's if you have enough! Don't nag your parents for money all the time, 'cause truly it doesn't grow on trees. Your parents are not your cash cows! Once you start earning and spending your own money, you might begin to learn how hard it is to look into an empty wallet, especially since it took you two hours cleaning tables or serving fast food to earn the money to spend at the movies. Learn to budget — that means working out what your expenses are, such as mobile phone, bus money, videos, going out with your friends, and even saving some for buying gifts at Christmas time. See JOBS.

MORALS = ethical beliefs, truths, virtues

Meaning

Oath

Responsible

Aspect

Lesson

Stable

(Something that you believe in ... and I don't mean Santa Claus!)

Everyone has morals and everyone's morals are different. For example, you may believe that you should wait to have sex with somebody until you both really love each other, but your friend might believe that it's OK to have sex with somebody just for the physical pleasure of it. That doesn't mean that you are right and she is wrong. Don't make judgements about people because they have different morals from yours; accept people for who and what they are.

MOVIES = films

Moving picture

Of

Visual

Images

Entertainment

Screen

(Popcorn and making out)

A good place to have a first date 'cause you don't have to do much talking! Movies are a great way to escape from your day-to-day life, and a lot of fun to watch, especially comedies.

OK, now we're going to talk about X-rated and porn films: X-rated and porn films. Talk over! ;-)

MUM = see FAMILY *(she's the matriarch!)*

MUSIC = tunes, melodies

Move your body

Underage disco

So alive

In time

Catchy tunes

(Makes your feet and fingers tap)

Listen to it whenever you can — R&B, Hip-Hop, radio, CDs, Latino, dance, cool bands and stuff. Is catchy, fun, cool and so alive. See CLUBBING and DISCO.

N

NAME-CALLING = see BULLYING
(because it's teasing)

NO! = not any, negative, denial, refusal

Not

On!

(The opposite of yes!)

No means no! Something that you need to say from time to time, even to your friends. Go with your gut feeling. If something doesn't feel right, say no and stick with your decision. You may not even have a good reason for saying no, but you don't have to explain yourself, just tell the truth: 'It doesn't feel right for now'.

O

ODOUR = smell, aroma, stink

Off

Deodorant-less

Obnoxious

Underarms

Reeking

(Eeewww … bad hygiene)

Man, if you've got bad hygiene, that's gross. Think of other people. But then maybe you don't realise you've got bad hygiene? Then I can bet you that people around you are giving you major hints about it. Ever heard them coughing as you walk closer? Or do they go blue in the face because they've stopped breathing when you're around? Odours come with the territory of growing up. You can't stop your body from sweating or growing hair but you can stop the odours becoming foul by showering or bathing daily, changing your clothes regularly and using anti-perspirants. Can't have too many deodorants ... one in your school bag, one at home, one in your sports bag, one in the car glove box. Just in case you're on your way to school and you remember you forgot to 'roll-on' before you left home. (Imagine if you didn't have one in the car or your school bag and you got to school and, 'Nnnoooooooooooo, I forgot to put on my deodorant,' and the weather is 45 degrees and getting hotter by the minute and you stupidly put on your long-sleeved school shirt which is like a sauna ... Well, just imagine ... Pugh ... I can smell you from here!). On a more pleasant note, there are some nice odours too — flowers, perfume, dinner cooking, clean guys, babies ...

OP-SHOPPING = see SHOPPING (same thing!)

OVERWEIGHT = see EATING DISORDER and BODY SHAPE (it's just weight, but a little more than what you should have)

P

PARENTS = fathers or mothers, guardians

Pushy

Ancestors

Responsible

Expectations

Naggy

Torturous

Suck

(Come on, they're not that bad. I'm a parent!)

I remember when I was a teen my mother used to say (after I'd given her a few more grey hairs), 'Wait until you have kids ... All the trouble you've given me you'll get back!' It's true. My son is a teen now and oh the joys ... *not*!

Remember this is a time when you are transferring from being a child to an adult, and your parents are also confused about the transition. How do they treat you now — as a child or an adult? The best thing for them to do is to try to combine both types of parenting by allowing you more responsibility to act like an adult but being there to support or guide you if your 'child' part slips up.

Anyhow, here are some 'pearls of wisdom' that I've learnt from being a parent *and* a daughter:

★ Communication works.

★ Parents make mistakes too.

★ They're older than you and think they know everything. I know, I know, my parents still do that to me and I'm nearly forty (ahem ... I mean twenty 8-))

★ Don't you hate it when you hear, 'When I was your age, ya-da, ya-da, ya-da'. Just pretend to listen and ignore it.

★ Even though you've had your seventeenth argument seventeen days in a row, they really do love you. It's not you they dislike, it's your behaviour.

★ Sometimes parents want you to do better than what they did, so they pressure you into becoming what they wanted to be. They can't 'make' you so don't get stressed out about it. Just try to see it from their side. It doesn't mean you have to follow their path.

★ Even though your mum can be your best friend, she is still your mum, and what she says goes.

★ Hating your parents is just a waste of time, especially if you've got a few years left to live with them. You have a choice: you either learn how to live with them and have a happy life or you choose to hate them and whinge and be bitter and twisted for the rest of your time at home. I know which one I'd prefer.

★ They learnt their parenting from their parents, and their parents learnt from their parents ... and so on.

★ Parents are like your personal bodyguards — they are on this earth to protect you.

★ Parents have issues of their own too. Remember the world doesn't revolve around you.

PARTIES = celebrations, functions

Pissed

Alcohol

Rage

Talent

Invitation

Excellent

Sex

(Socialising, flirting, guys and getting all dressed up)

Bet you get really upset if you miss out on one? Bet your parents use parties as bribes, like, 'Don't talk to me like that, young lady, or you won't be going to that party tonight!' Parties can be fun unless you drink too much (see ALCOHOL). They are usually only spoilt by gatecrashers — dickheads who you didn't invite to your party; the police — who turn up 'cause the neighbours complained about the loud music; parents — who come home early from wherever; drink or drugs — if the party gets out of control 'cause everyone's drunk and acting way too stupid or, even worse, somebody is doing drugs and has an allergic reaction and you have to call an ambulance …

Oh, the good old days of having a birthday party where everyone dressed as fairies and a clown came and we had sparklers on the cake and … get over it!

PASHING = see KISSING *(mmmmmm ...)*

PEERS = classmates, friends, people of the same age

Pressure

Equals

Encircling

Rank

Same age

(Are fun to hang around with)

But not cool if they pressure you. Don't do stuff because they want you to, or because you'll get your friends' approval. If you do, that's giving into 'peer pressure'. Are you doing stuff like smoking, having sex, shoplifting, drinking or doing drugs to fit in with a group? Have a think ... do you want to be you or do you want to be them? Dare to be yourself!

PERIODS = particular portions of time, cycles

Pain

Every month

Regular

Irritable

Overactive hormones

Date-killers

Sore boobs

(Name for that thing that happens every month)

Can happen any time between the ages of nine and sixteen, averaging about age thirteen. Just in case you were wondering, no — guys don't have to have them! OK, let's get into the gross part. You're not actually bleeding when you have a period. What's happening is that each month the uterus forms a lining made up of tissue and blood and then at a certain time of the month it lets it out, thus the wonderful thing called menstruation (periods). Get used to them, accept them as a part of your womanhood because the good news, girls, is that they don't just happen once (as some girls believe) but you will have periods every month until the average age of fifty-one! (Yep, I'm half way there … yeeeha!)

If you are having a lot of crampy pain or you think that you are bleeding too heavily, or there are lots of blood clots, please talk to an adult you feel comfortable with, because there are lots of methods of easing this time for us girls nowadays. The colour of the menstrual blood also varies from pink to dark shades of brown, sort of like paint colour selections. It's really important to shower regularly when you have your period, and change your pads or tampons regularly, then there won't be any noticeable smells — oh, the joys!

The most embarrassing thing about having your periods has to be if your pad or tampon leaks and you are walking backwards and sideways like a crab so nobody will notice the stain on your school uniform. If it happens, it happens! My trick at school was to cue my friend into checking the back of my school uniform every time we had to stand up! Another hint to avoid staining or noticeable stains is to wear black pants or skirts when I have my period and to line my underwear with heaps of panty liners for that stray blood that insists on leaking onto everything but the pad. Sounds wacky but it works!

PERSONAL POWER = see PEERS, BELIEVE IN YOURSELF, SELF-ESTEEM, GOALS and TRUST

PICK-UP LINES = (PICK UP) lift, get; (LINES) sayings, measures of poetry or songs

Pathetic

Idiotic

Conversations

Kick ass

Upsetting

Prude

Like

I'm

Naturally

Ever so

Stupid … not!

(Like, 'Did you just fall down from heaven?' Blech!)

Yep, corny is the word I use for pick-up lines. Sometimes they're cute, sometimes they're really sick. It can be flattering, but don't you wish the guy would just talk to you without having to think up some pathetic line? Unless he's drop-dead gorgeous and anything that comes out of his mouth is like melted white chocolate … dream on! So here's some advice:

★ If you don't like the guy who used the pick-up line, the standard thing is to roll your eyes and say, 'Whatever.' (see WHATEVER!)

★ If you think the guy's a hottie you giggle, inch a little closer to him and flutter your eyelids and he's all yours, baby!

PIERCING = drilling, punching holes

Puncture

Infection

Ear

Regrets

Cut

In tongue

Nipple

Groovy

(Punching holes in your body like a hole puncher in paper)

Getting stuff pierced is one of your parents' worst nightmares. They'd be cool with ears, but then when you start saying you want three in your right ear and six in your left ear and hey, a belly-button ring would be cool ... Nipple rings, eyebrow, tongue — anywhere that has a flap or a bulge! Piercing can be cool but if you get addicted to it, you'll start to look like a paper-clip holder and you'll beep like crazy when you go through a metal detector. Think about the reason you are having a piercing. Is it because you genuinely like it? Peer pressure? Or is it because you feel like rebelling and nobody can stop you having a piercing or tattoo 'cause it's your body and nobody can take it away from you? It's a personal thing but be sure about what you're doing.

At least you can take rings and bolts and stuff out and let the hole close over. But tattoos are more permanent. Do you really want 'I love Rick' on your bum when you're fifty and married to Jason? (Well, you could always name one of your kids Rick and pretend it was for him ... Yeah, right!)

PIMPLES = see ACNE *(same thing)*

PLUCKING = see SHAVING *(just as annoying)*

POLICE = see CRIME *(they come onto the scene if you're caught)*

POPULARITY = See COOLNESS and WANNABES *(they think they're popular!)*

PREGNANT = carrying foetus in womb

Preventative

Radiate

Expecting

Gestation

Nervous

Anxious

Nappies

Transform

(A direct sperm missile hit resulting in the target egg abandoning the others and going it alone … thus, baby making!)

Pregnancy can be a beautiful thing to experience, but maybe not when you are a teen who has major plans for your life. If you are intending to have sex and you have no intention of falling pregnant then you should study up on contraception. Don't assume that it's the guy's responsibility and he'll always have the condoms! Even with heavy making out you have to be really careful, 'cause if those little buggers (sperm) get anywhere near your vagina (and fertilise an egg), you may possibly be saying, 'Hello, Junior', in nine months.

I suppose you know the symptoms of being pregnant? The usual: missing period, tiredness, nausea and stuff. If you suspect that you might be, you can buy tests from your local chemist or even visit your doctor to have a proper test.

So, if you do accidentally fall pregnant, you're probably really scared. You've got to tell someone, especially an adult. If you can't go to your parents, talk to an aunt or family friend who will help you. If you don't have anybody to go to, there's heaps of help. Just look in the phone book — there are trained counsellors who will help you decide what to do. Don't go through this alone. You have many choices. Hey, and don't forget the guy you had sex with — he'll be the father, as much a part of this as you are.

PROBLEM-SOLVING = (PROBLEM)
complication, dispute; (SOLVING)
answering, explaining, working out

Predicament

Resolve

Overwhelmed

Brainstorm

Listen

Examine

Mediate

Solution

Outrage

Logic

Viewpoint

Idea

Neutral

Genius

(Putting out little fires, making decisions and sorting out stuff)

Problems and difficulties will always be there in your path as you grow. It's how you react and handle them that makes the difference. You are intelligent. You can solve your own problems and make your own decisions. Some will be right, some wrong — that's part of your journey. Don't be afraid to ask questions. When you need to make a decision and you're not sure, try to have some quiet time and meditate. If you bring yourself into a serene place in your imagination and ask yourself for an answer, you'll get it! (Sounds smarmy, but it works!)

PUNISHMENT = see CRIME *(what comes after you commit a crime)*

Q

QUESTIONS = see PROBLEM-SOLVING *(and then you'll get answers)*

QUIET TIME = (QUIET) peaceful, serene, hushed; (TIME) date, period

Quietness

Undisturbed

Inaudible

Ease

Tranquil

Term

Interval

Meditate

Era

(A good time to reflect)

This is *you* time. Time to gather your thoughts, time to process an event or the day. You can't process or gather your thoughts and feelings if you are with people, watching TV or on the phone all the time. Meditation is a great way to spend your quiet time. And it's not just sitting with your legs crossed, holding your palms up and humming. It's a time to shut your eyes and think about something or contemplate your next move in a situation. Meditating helps you make decisions or solve problems. See PROBLEM-SOLVING.

R

RAPE = violation

Ravish

Assault

Penetration

Endanger

(When you are forced to have sex with someone)

Rape is a criminal act and is not on! It's a horrible experience that no one should be put through. There are many ways of being raped and there are different types of rapists. Rapists can be total strangers, family members, neighbours or the guy at the local video store, or you can be out on a date and the guy forces himself on you, or it can even be your boyfriend! Yes, if you guys are in the middle of heavy stuff and even if he's about to you know ... put his thing in ... and then all of a sudden you change your mind and say, 'No!' but he just keeps going all the way, then that's rape too!

Girls who have been raped sometimes feel guilty, like somehow it's their fault. It isn't. You didn't 'ask for it' and you didn't 'dress for it' and you definitely didn't consent to it, so it's a crime. If you or a friend have been raped, you need to get medical attention immediately, as much as you feel disgusting and want to have a shower/bath, don't, as it can wash away evidence. It's very important to the police that you report to them immediately. Don't be scared of the reporting, the police call in counsellors and nurses to help you through it. You need to feel safe again, so it may take a while with counselling and stuff. You will get through it and get on with your wonderful life.

REBELLIOUS = disobedient, defiant

Rebel

Extreme

Behaviour

Endless

Lies

Leaving home

Insolent

Obstinate

Unruly

Selfish

(Going against anything your parents or school say)

Rebellious behaviour can be a pattern that you find hard to break. Sometimes you don't even know why you're going against the rules but you won't have anyone telling you what to do. Yeah, it can be cool to do what you want and sometimes you get a real rush from it, but there are rules and there are consequences. Rules are created for safety and protection, personal safety, community safety and world and environment protection. If we break rules, we not only put ourselves at risk but other people too. Our behaviour always has an effect on others. Before having a 'rebellious' moment, just think about who and what it may affect.

RELATIVES = see FAMILY *(same thing)*

RELAXATION = see QUIET TIME, SHOPPING, MOVIES etc. *(they all help you relax)*

RELIGION = faith, spiritual beliefs

Reverent

Explore

Love

Individual

God

Inspiration

Opinion

Neutral

(A spiritual force that you believe in)

It doesn't matter what religion you are, what matters is that you believe or have faith in something that is there for when you are feeling down or in need and can ask for help or guidance. Most people go through the stage of denying religion, especially if it was shoved down their throats as kids. As young adults you start to question your beliefs — this is normal. Just remember to respect other people and what they believe and don't try enforcing your own beliefs or non-beliefs on them. Spirituality is a part of you, find it within you.

REPORT CARD = written statement of school progress

Record

Evaluation

Parents

Outstanding

Review

Teacher

Communicate

Account

Relay

Document

(A sheet of paper that can ruin your life!)

Don't you feel like hiding your report card some-times? Especially when you know you worked damn hard the whole time and you still only got a C for Maths. I believe that, if that was the best you could do, then that's the best you can do!

When everyone compares their reports it often seems that if you have As all over the place you are the best, but that's not how we should judge each other.

Some parents put a lot of pressure on their kids to get As, so they can feel proud and brag to their friends and stuff. And some parents bribe or punish their kids for better or poor grades — that's so unfair. Everyone has their strengths and weak-nesses. You may be brilliant at Art and Drama, but struggle in Maths and Science — big deal! It really only matters when it comes to the subjects you need for your career. As long as you are doing well in the subjects relevant to what you want to do, keep going and celebrate the great grades. That doesn't mean that you just forget about Maths and Science — you still should do your best — but you may need to sit down with your parents and explain this to them. Like I've said before, some parents try to live their lives through their kids, so you need to understand their point of view.

RESPONSIBLE = accountable, dependable, trustworthy

Reliable

Extraordinary

Sensible

Power

Obliging

No nonsense

Stable

In charge

Bound

Liable

Example

(Being responsible for your own actions)

Yeah, that's right ... Personal responsibility! You are responsible for you, your thoughts, your words and your actions. But because you are still under the care of your parents, they are responsible for your welfare. Basically they have to legally provide you with shelter, food, clothing and an education. But you have to do the rest. When you want to do something your parents aren't too sure about, try not to say things like, 'But I'm responsible', or 'You have to let me have more responsibility'. That's not going to work. You have to show that you are responsible first, then your parents will let you be more independent. Taking responsibility isn't an easy thing. Empowerment and self-satisfaction come with it, but so do stress, consequences and disappointments.

And don't go blaming other people for how you feel or what you think about yourself — you can change your thoughts and actions and be what you want to be ... personal responsibility!

RESUME = see JOB *(you need one to apply for a job)*

REVENGE = see FORGIVE *(especially if after that huge talk on forgiveness you are still thinking of so-and-so who stole your boyfriend and felt happy visualising her fifty kilos heavier and with chickenpox all over her face! Tsk tsk ... 8-)*

ROMANCE = passionate relationship

Roses

Object of affection

Moon

Affair

Nice as

Charm

Exciting

(Love is in the air ...)

Those yummy feelings (not to be confused with lust for sex) that run through your body when you see or think about that special someone, and you want to do nice things for or with that person, like:

★ Buy them flowers (yes, girls can give guys flowers).

★ Hold hands walking along the beach.

★ Give them a spontaneous kiss in an elevator.

★ Make out in the back row of the movies.

★ Share your favourite food with them — yes, even chocolate!

★ Cuddle up on the couch with a blanket and watch videos.

★ Buy a special card that says something cute for no particular occasion and post it to them.

★ SMS them a spontaneous message like 'finkin of u'.

ROSES = see ROMANCE *(very romantic to receive them)*

RULES = see REBELLIOUS *('cause it leads to breaking rules)*

RUMOURS = see GOSSIP *(both negative talk)*

RUN AWAY = (RUN) escape, flee; (AWAY) elsewhere

Race off

Upset

Not here

Apart

Worry

Absent

Yonder

(Running away from home)

There are times when things get so bad at home that you just feel like getting out and running away from it all. But that won't get rid of the problem, it comes with you. The wise choice is to stay put and try to sort out the problem. Running away isn't as exciting as it sounds or looks on TV. It's a dangerous world out there if you have no money, no support and nowhere to sleep. What's the worst that can happen if you face up to the problem?

The best choice if you are in a situation you think is hopeless is to give one of the counselling centres a call, like Kids Helpline. If you *really* have to get out of the house, go to a friend's for the night, but make sure your parents know where you are. Making them worry about you may seem like the best revenge, but it's really cruel.

You'll come through it in the end, the rainbow always comes out after the storm.

S

SAD = see LONELY and DEPRESSION *(sadness is the basis)*

SCHOOL = a place for education, teaching or instruction

Sux!

Children

Homework

Order

Obey

Learn

(That place you have to drag yourself to every day)

Teachers, principal, homework, exams and stuff. Oh well, dat's life. Don't you just love looking back at your old school magazines? It's where you will get your education about life, friendships and your future. Yeah, but still they don't teach you this other stuff there, do they?

SCREW UP = see APOLOGY *(screwing up is making mistakes which can require an apology)*

SECRET = hidden, private

Safe

Exchange

Concealed

Recount

Ethics

Trust

(Stuff you don't want anyone to know … maybe just your best friend)

It's OK to have secrets, either between you and others or just with yourself, but there are secrets and then there are *secrets*. If you are holding onto a secret that is about you or somebody who may be in danger, then you can break that 'keeping a secret' code and tell an adult. Just remember that there aren't many people who you can trust with your secrets, see GOSSIP.

SELF-ESTEEM = cherishing self, being fond of self

Self

Expressed

Love

Forever

Expression

Self-image

Thinking positive

Enjoy being you

Ego

Maniac!

(Is when you love yourself! Not the 'she's got a big head' love yourself, but the 'I'm happy with who I am' love yourself)

You can't just go up to the chemist and say 'Oh, I want to feel confident today — think I need some self-esteem. Do you have the instant spray bottle in stock?' Self-esteem doesn't magically appear at the click of your fingers either. It is always deep inside you. You are what you think you are and you are what you say you are. So if you think positively about yourself and say great things to yourself you will have great self-esteem. If you keep criticising yourself as being dumb or unattractive then that's what you are telling your mind, in turn your mind will tell your body these negative things and it will show in your body language, facial expressions and speech.

Self-esteem and confidence come across loud and clear from somebody who is comfortable with themselves.

Tell your mind that you are smart and beautiful — it will tell your body the same and 'poof' — an intelligent and beautiful person will magically appear! Now go and look in the mirror, look yourself in the eyes and tell yourself how beautiful you are — and that you love you! Now! I know it sounds dumb and it's really hard to do if you don't believe what you're saying to yourself, but try it ... look in the mirror and repeat after me ... 'I love you! You are a beautiful person.'

Go ... Do it now! I'm not joking!

I'm waiting ... (SEX will have to wait) ... Waiting ... waiting ... I know you haven't done it yet ... What have you got to lose? If you think it's silly, laugh it off and just do it anyway!

Phew! Finally!

OK, was it as bad as you thought it would be? Did you vanish in a puff of smoke or disappear into a huge crack in the earth? Nah ... see — now let's move on.

SEX = intercourse, love making

Sex (might as well stick to the topic!)

Exs (you might have had sex with them?)

Xes (sex spelt backwards!)

(SEX SEX SEX SEX SEX)

Yeah, right, like I'm going to tell you about sex! Go and read someone else's book! ... You still here? Oh, do I have to? (Groan.) OK, here we go ... The birds and the bees, the flowers and the trees, yah-da, yah-da, blah, blah, blah, and that concludes our talk about sex for today, thank you. 8-)

Seriously, what can I say about it that you don't already know? There are so many different types of sex so I do recommend that you read lots of literature on it if you are curious. OK, but here are some extra hints that you need to hear again ... and again:

★ Don't be forced into it if you aren't ready.

★ Take precautions. Yes, that means you don't want to get pregnant.

★ Don't allow yourself to be in a situation where you don't have much control over your choices — that means alcohol.

★ Don't have sex because you want guys to like you — that's a SELF-ESTEEM problem.

★ Hey, let's not forget those gross diseases, and that doesn't mean that you can 'tell' if he's got a sexually transmittable disease because his penis is supposed to look like an ork's face, nah ... there are some diseases that are 'invisible', that means internal, and how would you know? Actually how would he know? Some people are carriers and it doesn't affect them at all.

Oh it's all too hard! Go with your gut feeling. You'll know when the time is right, and that doesn't mean when all your girlfriends have done it, it means right for you! Don't fall for the stories that guys give you to convince you to have sex with them. Don't confuse love and sex at your age. A guy saying he loves you just before he's trying to convince you to have sex is translated in a very basic way: 'I'm just trying the 'I love you' 'cause I want sex and you'll probably do it if I say it!'

You have the power to decide whether you are ready for sex or not. My final words: it's nicer and means more when you love the other person and they love you — aw, dat's cute!

SHAVING = cutting closely, trimming

Shaving cream

Hot wax

Apparatus

Vanishing requires

Implements that

Nicks &

Grazes

(Once you start you can't stop ... just like eating chocolates, but less enjoyable!)

Body hair sux. I can tell you, if you've got dark hair you're going to want to get rid of it in most places! You pluck, it comes back. You pluck, it comes back ... damn annoying! When you win the lotto get everything lasered, it's the futuristic version of plucking and it doesn't grow back! I can never understand why blondes shave or pluck, you can hardly see their hair. You don't have to use the shaving method, you can pluck or use removal creams or you can even bleach! (See, I told you, don't know why blondes bother. We even try to bleach our leg hair blonde to look like them!)

SHOPPING = buying, seeking things to buy

Shops

Habit

Op-shops

Pleasure

Purchasing

Important

Necessary

Great therapy

(Can't survive without it … it's a girl thing)

Yay, I love shopping! Who doesn't? Well, guys aren't too keen, but then there are some really spesh ones out there who will tag along to the shops or markets with you and actually enjoy it — and they're not necessarily gay (that's meant to be a compliment to gay guys)! Shopping, especially clothes shopping, always makes you feel that tiny bit better about yourself. Then you get home and check out your outfit in the mirror and then you create a party or outing just so you can wear your new clothes!

Op-shopping sounds kinda pov, but if you look carefully and mix and match you can find heaps of really good bargains!

Hang on, shopping means you need money ... here comes the old 'get a job' lecture ... Yawn!

SHOW-OFF = exhibitionist

Showy

Haughty

Outward

Walking advert

Overdoing it

Flaunt

Fake

(No one likes a show-off)

There's always one in the crowd trying to get all the attention either by yelling out answers to impress the teacher or dressing way too 'out there' on free clothes day or telling you (in their loudest voice so everyone can hear) how Mummy and Daddy took them to Switzerland for the weekend just to buy Swiss chocolate! Yeah, right!

You've got to feel a bit sorry for people who big-note themselves. They have little self-esteem and get off on telling everyone how good they are — sad.

SINGLE = alone, unattached, unmarried

Solo

Individual

Nab

Going it alone

Lone

Exclusive

(Me, myself and I)

Being single is when you're not going out with anyone. There are advantages and disadvantages. You can sometimes feel lonely and crave male intimacy or miss having a cute guy to go out with who knows every cute little thing about you. On the other hand you can have lots of fun being single by going out on lots of dates, flirting and meeting all sorts of guys and not having to answer to any of them.

Don't just date someone 'cause all your friends have got boyfriends and you feel a bit left out. Make sure you only make yourself non-single because you want to be with that person, not because it's the latest craze. And if you find that you go from boyfriend to boyfriend because you don't like to be alone, you need to ask yourself why? You also need to read LONELY.

SLEAZE = see CREEP *(both seedy guys)*

SLUT = immoral woman

Sordid

Loose

Unruly

Tart

(Someone you don't want hanging around your man!)

I couldn't find anything about sluts in any 'teen guides', but here goes ... my perception of a slut is a girl who has set low standards for herself by sleeping around and not having self-respect. Your interpretation may be entirely different. We aren't here to judge people who have different morals and values from ours, it's their choice, of course. If you know a 'slut' (though I really don't like the word — it's degrading and nobody deserves to be called it), you may even be able to look at her life, background and have some empathy for her and more understanding of why she is who she is. It's almost certainly another case of low SELF-ESTEEM.

SMOKING = puffing

Stinky

Mouth

Off

Kissing

Inhaling

Nicotine

Gum

(Inhale and expel tobacco smoke via your lungs)

Smoking just makes you sick — I won't go into the health problems. Just look around and you can see the results in people who have smoked for a long time. I know it may look cool — hey, I've done it too — but really what are we doing, inhaling poisonous (nicotine) smoke into our lungs? It would be healthier to stand next to an incinerator or a BBQ and inhale the smoke! What do we get out of it? Stinky breath, sore throat, stingy eyes, burnt holes in our clothes, smelly hair and clothes and yellow teeth! MMMmmm that's definitely gonna make me go out to buy a packet tomorrow ... not!

If you feel that you're addicted, then there's heaps of stuff to help you get off them, and if you feel you go from cigarettes to food, then you have an anxiety problem where you actually need to do something because you're worried or stressed. There are healthier ways to deal with worry and stress, like counselling and relaxation techniques. Oh yeah … kissing a smoker when you're a non-smoker is the biggest turn-off.

SOUL MATE = (SOUL) spirit; (MATE) companion

Spiritual

One and only

Union

Life

Match

Adrift

Team

Essence

(Two people who are made for each other)

You may or may not believe that there is a soul mate out there for you. You hear people sighing 'He's my soul mate …' and then going all ga-ga. Sometimes you have to wonder if they are just blinded by love or if it really could be possible. To me soul mates are two souls who are meant to be together and meet up lifetime after lifetime. Pretty far-fetched, considering the world population. But if it's possible, what is the key to finding that person who you are meant to be with? Does fate bring you together? If it does, how do you know you are soul mates? And then what? How many times do you keep meeting up and why? (I can hear the spooky music playing in the background ...)

SPUNK = see BOYS and MALE BODY *('cause they're all yummy)*

STALKING = pursuing, following

Shadow

Track

Abduct

Locate

Keen

Intrusion

Nuisance

Gross

(Scary stuff when someone is hunting you like an animal)

A stalker is someone who is obsessed with you and follows your every move. Stalkers can be male or female. They have psychological problems and it's not really about you. It can start with a friendship, a smile or a quick chat. Then suddenly you are the 'one', they become fond of you and literally can't get you off their mind. Then when they find their 'obsessiveness' isn't returned they start to get angry. So if a guy is carving your name into his arm, I'd start to get worried.

Sometimes a stalker isn't someone you know — it can be a total stranger who has picked you (yes, you lucky person) to stalk. They may start with watching you walk home from your bus, then they know where you live, then they know where you work, then they know your friends, then somehow they find out your name and phone number and it goes on and on.

If you think you are the victim of a stalker you need to report it to your parents, school and the police. Don't think it's going to go away — stalkers eventually have to be stopped and helped with their problem.

STEP-PARENT = (STEP) level, degree; (PARENT) mum or dad

Step-family

Threatened

Empathise

Parenting

Pain

Attention

Remarried

Ease into it

Neutral

Together

(A person who marries one of your parents)

With the divorce rate being so high, step-parents are becoming common and, as kids, we had fairy stories about wicked stepmothers shoved down our throats. I'm not saying that having a step-parent is all chocolates and roses (I wish), but if your parent chooses to move on with their life then it will affect you and you have to make the best of it.

If you start with a negative attitude towards your parent dating or remarrying, then it's your issue. Nobody will replace your mother and father, and I can tell you, your step-parent is not even trying to do this. They just fell in love with your parent and want to be happy with them. It can be a pain when the step-parent comes armed with six other kids, but you have to 'go with the flow'. You can't stop it happening, you have to try to work around the situation and find ways to cope with it all. Counselling, talking to other kids with stepfamilies and making sure you have time to yourself at home are great ways to cope.

I'm not saying that you always have to 'put up with it' — if you are literally being abused or mis-treated. You have the right to be safe. But if you are just trying to be difficult because you want your parents to get back together then you are making life hard for yourself.

STRESS = anxiety, pressure, burden

Strain

Tension

Restless

Emphasis

Scream

Snowball

(Some teenagers feel this angst 24/7!)

I believe stress is real, though some people think it's crap. It does exist but everyone deals with it differently and has different tolerance levels. Some people explode, have an outburst or get sick, which is what I call a 'meltdown'. Your levels get so high that your brain can't cope with them, so it shuts down and sends them down to your body. The key to dealing with stress is to control the levels. Picture your stress as being the mercury in a thermometer. When you feel your levels going up, try to use strategies to bring them down. Strategies like time-out, meditating, watching your favourite TV show, spending time with friends, having a bath, listening to music, writing in your diary, basically anything that helps you to relax (apart from drugs, alcohol and cigarettes ... please!) If you have a stressful period in your life, like exam time, just take things one step at a time, be organised and remember that all will be OK in the end.

Worrying is a waste of time — your mind's doing lots of gymnastics for what? You have control over your mind so you control your worries. You choose whether to worry or not. Break the worry cycle and live with less stress. Just ask yourself, 'What's the worst that can happen?' and live life to the full.

STUDY = see EXAMS *(you have to do this before you sit for that)*

SUICIDE = see DEPRESSION *(depression can be the first sign)*

SWEARING = cursing, blasphemy

Shocking

Words

Exclaim

Abuse

Rage

Insults

Not nice

Gross

(Like, swearing and shit. Oh, oops …)

I suppose swearing is an everyday part of high-school language. For some, swear words have become a habit; others use them to shock; and then there are those who are only triggered into using swear words when they're really pissed off! It's a personal choice, but many people, especially teachers, don't like it.

T

TALENT = gift, ability, brilliance

Truly
Artistic
Lone
Expert
Naturally
Talented

(If you've got 'it', you've got it!)

Everyone has a talent. It can either be with dance, acting, designing, singing, computers, public speaking, mathematics, or even creative writing (cough, cough). And it can be something different that you can do that nobody else can, like the way you file your stamps in your stamp album or the way you can just grab a microphone and talk your head off without getting nervous.

If you have low self-esteem you won't believe in your talent. Just listen to people around you. If you're getting a lot of, 'You're so good at that!' believe it, embrace it and nurture it.

TAMPONS = plugs of cotton wool *(seriously — that's what the dictionary said!)*

Tubes

Awkward

Muscles

Periods

Overflow

Nervous

Sanitary product

(Those things that idiot-guys find fascinating when they run them under water, watch them swell up then chuck them at us girls when we walk past!)

Tampons are great when you want to swim or exercise when you have your period. If you've never used them before you may want to have a few practices and it may hurt the first couple of times, until you get used to inserting them. You might want to talk to an adult or friend before you start using them and, just like pads, they need to be changed regularly. It's not a good idea to keep them in at night either. You may even find the ones with an applicator easier to use. My advice: read the instructions carefully.

TANNING = see BEACH ('cause that's where you get a tan)

TEACHERS = see SCHOOL *(yep, without them school would be cool)*

TEARS = see DEPRESSED and BREAK-UPS *(lots of crying happens with these things)*

TEENAGER = see YOUNG ADULT *(that's what you are)*

TELEPHONE = see MOBILE PHONE *(we use both way too much!)*

TIRED = see HEALTH *(if your health isn't that great, then you'll feel tired)*

TRUST = confidence, certainty

Truly

Rely

Upon

Sharing secrets

Two-faced

(Go with your gut feeling)

Trusting yourself is more important than trusting somebody else. Trust yourself to make the right decisions for yourself; go with your gut feelings.

TRUTH = true facts, actual

True

Real

Uncompromising

Trusty

Honesty

(Pinocchio had a little problem with it)

What's the truth? There's so much going on out there that sometimes the truth can be hiding behind masks. Just be true and honest with yourself and others. But sometimes 'the truth hurts', so use your gut feeling when you are speaking the truth. Sometimes it may be hurtful to the other person, but that's not your problem. Don't invent anything to make them feel better about themselves, that's not your responsibility. And ask that people do the same with you — speak the truth, that is.

TWO-FACED = see GOSSIP and TRUST
(some people play both sides)

U

UNDERWEAR = see BRAS and G-STRINGS
(those things you wear under clothes)

UNFAITHFUL = see CHEAT *(same thing —
both not good!)*

UNHAPPY = see LONELY and DEPRESSION
*(well, when you put the UN in front of
HAPPY it means the opposite, not happy)*

UNI = college, school of higher or tertiary
education

Unlimited subjects

Novice again

Institute of education

(Starting school again)

Uni isn't like the seventies films where everyone is high, lying around making out on the grass, skipping classes and stuff. University is great and a lot of fun. But it's also a lot of hard work and a major challenge. Also a great experience dealing with new faces and a different education style. If you're not ready for university, that's fine — you always have the opportunity to go to Uni at a later stage. Hey, look at me! I didn't go to Uni for the first time until I was thirty-five!

UNTIDY = messy

Unorganised

Neat … *not!*

Teens

Inhabit

Disorderly

Your room

(Not every teen's bedroom looks like a bomb hit it!)

You are either a tidy person or an untidy person.

Tidy = Your room looks like it's straight out of a décor magazine, you know where everything is, you have everything labelled and colour co-ordinated (and now we're starting to think that you are overdoing the tidy thing and you need to get a life!).

Untidy = You can't open the door 'cause of the pile of clothes blocking the doorway, you can't find your jeans, your new top, your sneakers … or anything else basically! You don't know what's clean or dirty 'cause *all* your clothes are strewn across the room. If you are tidy, then move on to V. If you are untidy read on …

Can't picture yourself as a tidy person? That's OK, but what about trying to find a balance? If you are interested in knowing how to be a little tidier, read on …

(I wonder if there's anybody left that's reading this? Ah well, just in case I'd better write something!) Basically, you need to get organised and it's not hard.

Here are a few hints:

★ Getting changed. Dirty? Put them straight in your laundry basket (get one if you don't have one). Clean? Hang them up or put them away.

★ Coming home from school. Do you normally throw your bag into a corner? That's fine, why don't you make it a 'school corner' where you do your homework and keep everything to do with school? Create a desk area and get some trays or baskets to throw paperwork and stuff in.

★ Have a basket or box in a corner for stuff that you can't be bothered putting away or finding a place for. Throw it in there and one day (one day ...) you'll sort through it. At least it's better in one place than all over your room.

★ Make your bed as soon as you get up in the morning, otherwise it becomes a great storage place to chuck anything onto.

If you get into these few habits, they'll just become a part of life and you won't even have to think about it, you'll do it automatically.

V

VALENTINE = chosen love interest on
St Valentine's Day

Violins

Affection

Love

Eternal

Nervous

Trusting

Infatuation

Noticeable

Emotions

(Cupid's day you wait for once a year)

It can be a surprise to find out who's got a crush on you! Some people see Valentine's Day as an opportunity to tell people they love them, others think it's crap and a total waste of money. If you are part of a couple and celebrate Valentine's Day, you would probably say it's the best. If you're single and don't even get a text message and you see all your friends get cards and flowers, then I'm sure you'll say it's all crap!

VANITY = see SHOW-OFF *(just a fancy word for showing off)*

VEGETARIAN = non meat/fish eater

Vegetable

Eating

Greens

Eggs

Tofu

Appetite

Rice

Ingredient

Alfalfa

Nourishment

(You don't have to be a hippie to be a vegetarian)

Not to be confused with a vegan, who doesn't eat meat, eggs or dairy products. It's cool to be vegetarian nowadays, 'cause there's heaps of good vego food available in stores and on menus. If you are thinking of becoming a vegetarian, do a little research and make sure you eat a balanced diet, taking in the nutrients that you would normally get from meat and fish.

VIOLENCE = see CRIME and ABUSE *(they're all illegal)*

VIRGIN = untouched, pure

Virtue

Immaculate

Resist

Girl/guy

Inexperienced

New

(A person who hasn't had sex yet)

Not only girls are virgins but guys are too! You can remain a virgin for as long as you want — it's your choice. You don't have to have sex if you don't want to. Make sure that your decision to have sex is *your* decision and that you feel comfortable with it. You would probably like your first time to be special, not rushed or pressured. Waiting until you feel ready is a really mature way of thinking. Just 'cause Barbie and all her friends got the latest pair of jeans doesn't mean you have to go out and get them too, you know! (Ah, Josie, what have jeans got to do with virgins?)

W

WANNABES (from WANT TO BE) = people who desire or crave to be like someone else

Wish

And

Need

Noticeable

Attention to

Be

Exactly

Same

(Female versions of JOCK)

Wannabes are 'try-hards' — people who aren't being themselves because they're spending so much time trying to be like someone else. There's usually a leader of the wannabes and she's usually the Queen Be. (Get it? Ha!) The wannabes just fuss all over her and idolise her (watch some of those 'prom queen'

American movies and you'll soon spot Queen Be
and her Wannabes —sounds like a singing group!)
It's pathetic, like ... Get a life!

WARDROBE = see CLOTHES *(yeah, yeah, I
know it's where you hang your clothes!)*

WAXING = see SHAVING *('cause they're both
a pain in the &%#)*

WEIGHT = see EATING DISORDER *(being
obsessed about your weight can be a trigger
to an eating disorder)*

WHATEVER! = no matter what, anything at all,
who cares?

When
Hard
Attitude
Takes
Every
Vanquish
Expressing
Response

(Is translated as, 'Yeah, right, I don't really want to hear what you're saying,' or, 'I don't agree with you but I think you're right and I'm not going to admit it and I don't give a @!#*!)

If you are going to use the term 'whatever' you have to do it properly. Here are my whatever instructions: Tilt your head to one side for two seconds and as you say, 'Whatever', wave your head from side to side like one of those jiggly animals that sit in the back of the car window. Remember to close your eyes for one second and, as you open them, roll them up. If you want an 'advanced whatever', hold your right hand out like you're signing *stop* and add, 'Talk to the hand 'cause the face ain't hearin' it!' Yeah, I know ... sounds very Rikki Lake and Jerry Springer, but hey, it works.

WITCHCRAFT = enchantment, magic, sorcery

Wizards/witches

Incense

Tools

Casting spells

Herbs

Crystals

Religion

Astrology

Fairies

Tarot

(Curses, spells, potions and stuff)

We may dabble in a little witchcraft, even if it's just tarot cards, crystals or reading how to cast love spells, but if you're going to be serious, then dabbling won't cut it. Witches are pagans and paganism is a religion. Because of the knowledge we now have, society doesn't feel the need to burn witches at the stake anymore! About time. Now, where's my broomstick?

WOBBLY BITS = (WOBBLY) quivery; (BITS) pieces

Waves

Outer

Blobby

Bits

Loose

You

Bum

Image

Twist

Shake

(Those wobbly parts of your body that create waves as you walk)

OK, I suppose I better talk about them … bums and wobbly bits, that is. Don't want to! (Only 'cause it's a real sore point, this subject.) Wobbly bits? Which bits are wobbly? There are too many bits of my body that are wobbly … OK, now I'm depressed (should go back and read my own advice)! See HEALTH. (Yes, Josie!)

X

X-PLANATIONS = see PROBLEM-SOLVING
(when you work out your problem you get an explanation)

X-RATED MOVIES = see MOVIES *('cause they're both on a screen)*

Y

YOUNG ADULT = (YOUNG) teen, not yet old; (ADULT) grown-up, mature

You

Are!

(Huh? So which is it? Teen? Or grown-up?)

Is this a glossy word for teenager? I think it's meant to make you feel more important and stuff. So when adults want to treat you like a kid and don't want you to go to that party, they say, 'But you're still just a teenager'. Then when they want you to be more responsible or do a job for them, they say, 'You're a young adult now, Johnny!' Grown-ups! You just can't please them.

YUPPIE = see WANNABES and JOCK ('cause they're all losers)

Z

ZITS = see ACNE *(the word ZIT isn't even in my dictionary! Who made that word up anyway?)*

ZONKED = see HANGOVER, ALCOHOL and DRUGS *('cause they all make you feel this way)*